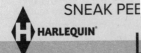

KISS

THE DOWNFALL OF A GOOD GIRL

Carpe diem. Be bad.

She couldn't regret the decision. She might not be able to say why she'd made that choice, but something about the feel of Connor's mouth on her neck, the caress of his hands under her jacket to the small of her back... It felt good. There was something liberating in this—more than just seizing the day. It was new and scary territory for her, but it felt right, too.

Connor loomed over her, those powerful arms bracketing her shoulders and holding him solid and steady, eyes hot on her body and face. When he finally met her gaze, she realized he was giving her one last chance to end this before it was too late.

"It's already too late," she whispered.

The corner of Connor's mouth curved up. "But I've only just begun."

DEAR READER,

Connor and Vivi's story took me to one of my favorite places on earth: New Orleans. This is a city that truly has something for everyone—history, music, food, architecture, art.... No matter your age or your interests, New Orleans delivers. I spent a lot of time there when I was in high school and college, and while there are many stories to tell, I must refrain. My mother is probably reading this, and ignorance is definitely her bliss.

I watched in horror as the levees failed in the wake of Katrina, and I worried how the city I loved so much would ever recover—and what would it be like when it did? Would a rebuilt New Orleans still have that unique culture and attitude that made it so special?

I should have known better. It would take more than a flood to erase the character of New Orleans. And its distinct flavor and attitude still permeate everything, practically making the city itself a character in any books set there. There's no place quite like it.

Between the actual characters, the *very* important, totally necessary trip to New Orleans for research and working with local singer-songwriter Cristina Lynn to create Connor's songs, I'm not sure which part of writing this book I enjoyed most.

But I do know that I'm thrilled that Connor and Vivi's story was chosen as one of KISS's debut titles! It's an honor, of course, to be asked to help launch a brand-new Harlequin series, but KISS is an awesome place for me to call home. I think KISS has some of the best authors in the Harlequin family in the line, and the stories they're writing put a fresh twist on category romance. It's very exciting to be a part of this!

I hope you enjoy *The Downfall of a Good Girl* and are looking forward to Lorelei's story, *The Taming of a Wild Child,* coming next month. There's nothing like a sultry New Orleans summer....

Geaux Saints!

Kimberly

P.S. Be sure to drop by my website at www.BooksByKimberly.com before the end of March—I'm celebrating the launch of KISS and the release of these books with some great contests.

THE DOWNFALL
OF A GOOD GIRL

KIMBERLY LANG

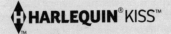

Recycling programs
for this product may
not exist in your area.

ISBN-13: 978-0-373-20701-5

THE DOWNFALL OF A GOOD GIRL

www.Harlequin.com

ABOUT KIMBERLY LANG

———

Kimberly Lang isn't one of those people who always knew she wanted to be a writer. She actually wanted to be a ballerina, but puberty failed to deliver the required swanlike elegance. That dream scuttled, she went on to get her master's degree in English—and she has the bartending skills to prove it. With the blessings of her family, she quit teaching in 2007 to write full-time, and in May 2008, sold her first book to Harlequin's London office. That book, *The Secret Mistress Arrangement,* debuted at number nine on the Borders Series Bestseller list and won the 2009 National Readers' Choice Award for Best First Book.

Since then, Kimberly's books have appeared on the *USA TODAY,* Amazon, Borders, Barnes & Noble and BookScan bestseller lists, and have been translated into more than a dozen languages. (And, yes, that's *really* cool.)

She's married to her college sweetheart, whom she affectionately (but appropriately) calls her Darling Geek, and is mom to the most brilliant and beautiful child on the planet. She teaches yoga-based fitness because she eats way too many jelly beans while writing and has found that spending time with her butt over her head helps spark her creativity. More than one sticky plot point has been solved in the Down Dog position. She has no hobbies because she doesn't have time, but if she did, they'd include knitting, skiing and ballroom dancing, because they sound as if they might be fun.

You can visit Kimberly's website at **www.BooksByKimberly.com** to learn more about Kimberly and her books.

This is my tenth book, a milestone
that I couldn't have hit without the continued love
and support of my family: Darling Geek, Amazing Child
and WonderMom. Y'all are the best.

But I want to extend a huge thanks to the talented and
delightful Cristina Lynn, who literally put a song on
Connor's lips by allowing me to use her lyrics in this
book. You can hear those songs—and a new one called
"Sinners and Saints" inspired by Connor and Vivi's
story!—by visiting her website at www.CristinaLynn.com.

THE DOWNFALL
OF A GOOD GIRL

ONE

—

Vivienne LaBlanc waited impatiently, trying not to bump her wings against anything or move too quickly in a way that would cause her halo to slide off, as Max Hale gave his introductory speech on the other side of the curtain.

"There are many krewes, but none like the Bon Argent. Five years ago, we decided to do something—in our own hometown style—to raise money for the victims of Hurricane Katrina. We were far more successful than we dreamed. Through the Saints and Sinners Festival—which grows bigger every year—we've raised hundreds of thousands of dollars for dozens of local charities, and I thank all of you for your continued support."

After a short round of polite applause, Max continued to laud their accomplishments, but Vivi listened with only half an ear. She was well aware of the great work of Bon Argent; she'd been involved with the krewe since its inception. Candy Hale was one of her oldest friends, and Max was like a second father.

Her mother used to serve on the board, for goodness' sake, so she didn't need to be sold on the success. She did, however, need a primer on these wings.

How am I supposed to sit in these things? The feathered and bejeweled wings were beautiful, arching up to head height and hanging to her calves. Vivi frowned as she tried to adjust the buckle on her gold sandals and felt the whole getup shift dangerously. Honestly, she looked less like a saint and more like a Vegas showgirl who'd crashed the neighborhood nativity play.

The Saints and Sinners ball—and the whole Bon Argent krewe—bordered on silly at times, but the costumes and the parody of pomp and pageantry was what had made the Saints and Sinners fundraiser so fun, popular and immensely successful in such a short time.

And there were three hundred people out there eagerly awaiting the announcement of this year's Saint and Sinner. Following the traditions of the traditional Mardi Gras krewes, those identities were top secret info. As far as Vivi knew, only three people were in the know this year. Max, the head of the Bon Argent charity, Paula, the head of PR, and Ms. Rene, the seamstress who'd made the costumes for the Sinner and the Saint. Even she didn't know who would be her other half between now and Fat Tuesday.

She had a few guesses in mind.

Unlike the traditional krewes, however, who would crown a king and a queen, Bon Argent had no gender requirements to fulfill. The Saint and the Sinner were chosen for their local celebrity and reputations and could be of the same gender. Vivi had her bets on nightclub owner Marianne Foster, who'd been in the news a lot recently and would provide excellent competition before Vivi crushed her. While Marianne would be popular in the voting and bring in large amounts of money, it wasn't an overstatement or egoism to say that she, herself, was *more* popular and could raise *huge* amounts of money in comparison.

She stomped down the unkind thought. Thoughts were the precursors to words and actions, and she'd learned to keep her head in the right place in order to avoid saying or doing anything she might regret later. *It's about the money we can raise, not about winning.*

But it was *also* about winning. The Sinner had taken the crown the last two years, but this year top honors were going to the Saint, because she simply refused to lose. She'd only lost one crown in her life, and she still remembered the bitter taste of watching Miss Indiana walk away with it. It didn't matter how much she liked Janelle personally, or what a great Miss America she'd turned out to be, it still sucked to lose.

So she was competitive. It was hardly a personality flaw. No one *liked* to lose. And in this case, her competitive nature would be beneficial because it was all for a good cause.

Max was now introducing her Cherubim Court: ten local high school kids chosen by the charity's board to be her team in the fundraising.

And now it was her turn. She took a deep breath, checked her dress, and waited.

"...my pleasure to introduce Saint Vivienne LaBlanc!"

The curtain opened to a strobe of flashes from the

photographers gathered in front of the stage and a very heartening roar of approval and applause from the guests. Vivi heard her sister's distinctive whistle and looked over at the table where her family sat. When she'd left the table twenty minutes ago, claiming she had an emergency phone call from the gallery, Lorelei had given her a knowing look. She waved as she watched people from the surrounding tables congratulate her parents.

Being chosen as the Saint was quite an honor, and Vivi was beyond touched by the applause that showed so many people thought her deserving of it. She'd won a lot of contests in her life, brought home quite a few crowns, but this was different. It wasn't about being pretty or popular. The downside to her pageant career was the assumption by all that she was just a pretty little face with no real substance. She'd spent years fighting that stereotype, trying to prove that there was more to her. It had been her biggest challenge to date, and the halo on her head was proof she'd succeeded. It might be cheesy and rather silly-looking, but it suddenly meant more to her than any crown she'd ever worn.

Beating the Sinner—whoever that turned out to be—would be icing on the cake at this point, and now she wanted that trophy more than anything.

Vivi removed her halo with the proper pomp, placing it on the blue satin pillow that would hold both the Saint's halo and the Sinner's horns until the competition ended and the winner claimed both trophies. She then took her seat with her court and applauded politely as the Sinner's court, the Imps, was introduced.

Max took a deep breath and looked so excited he might burst with it. "Our Sinner this year is an obvious choice, and we're so pleased he's made time in his schedule to reign over this important event."

The pronoun usage told Vivi that she'd lost her bet. Damn, she'd been so sure it would be Marianne. *It doesn't really matter,* she thought with a mental shrug. She was ready to take on anyone.

"...Connor Mansfield!"

Vivi's smile froze as the crowd broke into wild applause. *You're freakin' kidding me.*

Connor caught a glimpse of Vivi's face as he stepped onto the stage and nearly laughed at the perfect mix of horror and fury against a feathery backdrop of angel wings. Not that he blamed her; his response had been very similar when he'd heard her name called, but he'd still been safely behind the curtain.

He had to hand it to the board of Bon Argent; they certainly knew how to guarantee maximum attention from the local press—attention that could be otherwise difficult to draw amid everything else happening during the Mardi Gras season. They'd probably break every fundraising record in history.

Vivi just looked like she'd like to wring his neck, but then she always looked at him like that. Some things just never changed, no matter how long you were gone from your hometown.

But the show must go on, and everyone was waiting for them to take their seats so dinner could be served. He removed his horns and solemnly placed them next to the Saint's halo. Then he walked over to

Vivi, nodded politely and waited for her to return the gesture. Slowly, they made their way to the high table. When they reached their seats a cheer went up from the crowd, and the competition of the Saints and Sinners Festival officially began. Servers appeared from the woodwork and the crowd turned its attention to the salad course.

He leaned a few inches in her direction. "You're going to ruin three years of orthodontic work if you don't stop grinding your teeth, Vivi."

Her eyes narrowed, but she released her jaw the tiniest bit. She reached for her wineglass, noticed it was empty and reached for a water glass instead. He saw her look at it carefully, then shrug before she drank. Knowing Vivi, she'd debated dumping it in his lap.

"I'd say Welcome Home, but—"

"But you wouldn't mean it." He grinned at her to annoy her.

"But," she corrected, "it would be rather redundant, considering the reception you just got."

"Jealous I got more applause?"

"No." She shifted in her chair. "I'm not an attention whore."

"Big talk from the pageant queen."

Vivi inhaled sharply and her smile became tight. "Some of us have outgrown our adolescence."

He pretended to think about that for a second, then shook his head sadly. "No, you're still sanctimonious."

"And you're still a—"

She stopped herself so suddenly Connor wondered if she'd bitten her tongue.

She inhaled sharply through her nose and swallowed. "You must be very pleased to finally be recognized for *your* achievements."

"I hate to burst your bubble, *Saint* Vivienne, but these titles aren't character references."

"Oh, really?" Vivi's face was the picture of confused innocence. "You seem to be perfectly suited for the title."

And there was the first dig. He should have known that Vivi wouldn't let that pass. Although he'd been vindicated, rumor and gossip had done their damage. Everyone believed there had to be a grain of truth in there somewhere—*which* grain it might be was the engine that drove the gossip that wouldn't die.

Vivi might have hit a sore spot with her first salvo, but damned if he'd admit that. "Sanctimonious *and* judgmental. You need to increase your repertoire."

"Maybe you should add some to yours, as well. A little decorum from you would be nice, considering the honor you've been given."

"According to you, it's not really an honor, now, is it?"

"Yet you still seem very pleased with yourself." She snorted. "You look ridiculous, you know. Black leather pants, Connor? Really? What is this? 1988?"

He'd had a similar thought when they'd been presented to him. "I agree on the pants. Very eighties glam metal. But then I guess it fits the costume."

Vivi smiled—a genuine one this time—at the server who filled her wineglass, but the smile disappeared as soon as the server did. "I don't know what Max was thinking," she grumbled at her salad. "The Saint and the Sinner are supposed to be *local* celebrities."

"I'm literally the boy next door, Vivi. I'm as local as you are."

"You *were* local," she corrected him. "Now you're international. You're off touring far more than you're in town."

He tried to get comfortable in his chair, but the enormous black wings attached to his back made that feat nearly impossible. He didn't quite understand the mixed-metaphor approach to Saints and Sinners, but Ms. Rene had gone for a Lucifer vibe. He felt more like a giant crow. "So it's the fact that my job requirements keep me out of town a lot that you object to?"

Vivi tried to brush her hair back over her shoulder, but it only got tangled in her wings, creating modern art-inspired shapes in the white feathers. She tugged at the strands as she spoke. "I object to the creation of an unlevel playing field."

Except for that jet-black hair, Vivi had the right looks to pass as an angel—wide blue eyes, fair skin, elegant features. The fire in her eyes was far from angelic, though. Irritation made her movements jerky, tangling her hair even worse.

"How is this unlevel in any way?"

With one final tug that probably pulled some of it out by the roots, Vivi finally got the last of her hair loose. A rhinestone from her wings, loosened in the tussle, fell into her cleavage. Vivi looked down briefly, and Connor's eyes followed hers to the valley of creamy skin before he snapped them back to her face. She had a beautiful mouth, lush and full and sinful—until she opened it and killed the illusion.

"Your groupies and your fan club and all your famous friends will make sure to fill your coffers so that you win."

"But that's what this is about, right? Raising money?"

"Of course that's what's important," she conceded through a jaw clenched so tight it had to be painful, "but you have an unfair advantage when it comes to the actual contest. No one could compete with you."

He grinned at her. "I'm glad to finally hear you admit it."

"I meant," she gritted out, "that I'm a hometown girl and you're a freakin' rock star. You have a bigger fan base by default and *that's* an unfair advantage."

"Your title is 'Saint', Vivi, not 'martyr'."

Vivi's knuckles turned white, and Connor expected the stem of her wineglass to snap at any moment.

"Just eat your dinner."

He shot her a smile instead. "You could just concede now, you know."

She choked on her wine. "Hell has not frozen over."

"So it's on?" he challenged.

"You're damn right it's on." Grabbing her fork, she speared her lettuce with far more force than necessary.

Vivi could never turn down a challenge. It didn't matter what it was, Vivi went after everything in her full-out, take-no-prisoners style. He actually respected that about her. It was one of the few things they had in common. Everything *else* about her, though, drove him insane. Always had.

He really shouldn't let Vivi get to him. He was an adult, for God's sake. Vivi might not like him, but plenty of other women did, so her holier-than-Connor attitude shouldn't bother him. There was something about her, though, that just crawled under his skin and itched.

Would he have agreed to do this if he'd known up front that Vivi would be a part of it? Or would he have just sent another check and let it go?

No, he'd been thinking about home for a while now; this was just the nudge he'd needed to get him here. It gave him an excuse to do some damage control, make some new headlines that didn't involve paternity suits or sexual activities. He could take a step back and maybe take a deep breath for the first time in years.

He hadn't realized how truly tired he was. Getting everything he'd ever wanted in life was great in theory, but he hadn't known he'd be left feeling like a well-dressed hobo. He had accepted that at first: he couldn't have gotten this far if he'd been tied down to any one place or thing. There was a great freedom to it. But it came at a cost, nonetheless.

Being home—really home, not just the place he slept between shows—made him feel like the earth was solid under his feet again. The ideas that had been swimming unformed in the back of his mind seemed to be taking shape now that he was here. New Orleans was good for his mind and soul, and he could use the next few weeks to really refocus and figure out what was next. Or what he wanted to be next.

He heard Vivi's deep sigh of irritation and it brought him back to the present. Right now he had a contest to win. It felt good to come home; even better to come home to a warm welcome *and* the opportunity to do something good for his hometown.

Annoying Vivi while he did it was just a bonus.

Vivi chewed each bite a dozen times and then immediately put another bite in her mouth to keep it full. She couldn't control her thoughts, but this was one way to guarantee she would not take Connor's bait and end up saying something she'd regret later.

This just sucked. She'd headed enough fundraisers to know that Connor was a gift from the fundraising gods. The money would pour in *and* the publicity would be unreal. The rational, reasonable part of her mind applauded Max Hale's choice and envied his ability to get Connor to agree to participate.

But Connor Mansfield? *Argh.* If she had to be paired with a musical superstar, why couldn't they have picked any one of the *other* dozens of musical legends who called New Orleans home? But, no, they had to get maximum mileage by bringing Connor in, especially since he was very much the biggest Sinner in the media right now.

From the top table she had an excellent view of the entire ballroom. The guest list was a Who's Who of New Orleans' rich and powerful, and she knew every face in the crowd. And everyone in the room knew damn well that they hated each other.

Hated was the wrong word. People liked to toss it around, but she didn't hate Connor. She disliked him a hell of a lot, but *hate* implied more energy than she was willing to commit. She and Connor were just not meant to occupy the same time-space continuum. Connor was the one person who could make her blood boil just by breathing. Any conversation was just asking for an anger-induced stroke.

She felt a headache forming behind her left eye.

From the looks being tossed their way, every person in that room knew exactly how much she hated being up here with Connor and found it endlessly amusing. There were probably bets being taken right this second that they'd witness a repeat of that ball ten years ago when the Queen had slapped the King ten minutes after their coronation.

Connor had completely deserved it, but it had taken her forever to live that down nonetheless. It had even come up a few months later, in her interview during the Mississippi River Princess pageant, with the implication that she had a penchant for making unseemly scenes that would be detrimental to the title. She'd learned quite a bit about handling herself and her image after that, so in an odd way Connor had helped fuel her pageant success. Still, that night had pretty much been the final straw, and she and Connor had kept a healthy distance from then on unless forced otherwise by circumstance.

But then Connor's music had started to take off, and he'd spent more time out of town than in it. Within a few years he'd become a rising superstar and their paths had ceased to cross entirely. Bliss.

She would console herself with the knowledge that Ash Wednesday was only four weeks away, and Connor would go back to Los Angeles or New York or wherever his home base was now, and her life would go back to normal. It was a small consolation, but consolation nonetheless.

Could she put up with him for that long? *Without* blowing her top? They were adults now: older, wiser, more mature. Maybe things could be different. She risked a sideways glance.

Probably not.

Everything about Connor projected smug arrogance. He was overly sure of himself, always seeming to have that mocking smile on his face as if he was laughing at her. Even sitting there, dressed like Lucifer on his way to a Pride parade, he still managed to look confident and cocksure.

Ms. Rene had put him in black leather—not only the pants she'd mocked him about earlier, but also a black sleeveless vest and motorcycle boots. Strips of studded black leather circled his biceps, drawing attention to the powerful bulges no one would expect a piano-playing singer to have.

It was a nice contrast to her all-white satin and feather combo. But where her costume veered to the demure and saintly, Connor's screamed *sex*: the leather fit him like a second skin, leaving little to the imagination. While Ms. Rene had covered every exposed inch of *her* skin with body glitter, Connor's skin had been oiled to give him an other-worldly sheen.

He was tall, dark and dangerous personified—from the dark hair that hung a little too long to the goatee that framed his mouth... She swallowed hard. Her love of art gave her an appreciation for beauty, but this was not just male beauty. There was virility, strength, passion. It was hard *not* to appreciate Connor on that level.

Connor looked up, caught her glance, and grinned a lady-killer smile that crinkled the corners of his rich brown eyes.

It was enough to melt any woman—at least until he opened his mouth.

"Problem, Vivi?"

"Just surprised by your goatee. Lose your razor while you were on tour?"

He rubbed a hand over it. "I thought it went with the costume. Maybe made me look a little devilish, you know."

"It's as ridiculous as the pants," she lied, and went back to her dinner. Connor looked devilish, dangerous, sexy and ready to steal a dozen female souls.

And the women probably wouldn't even put up much of a fight. Women loved Connor.

Who was she kidding? *Everyone* loved Connor, praised his talents, celebrated his success. That was one of the reasons why everyone made such a big deal out of the fact that she didn't.

She wasn't a hundred percent sure why or how it all started, but in the twenty-five years she'd known Connor she couldn't remember a single time when he had not irritated her to the point of justifiable homicide.

And it wasn't like she was evil. She *liked* people. Connor was the only person on the planet who affected her in that way, and she dealt with all kinds of irritating people all the time. She was known for her people skills. Those skills just didn't extend to cover annoying man-child rock stars.

As he'd said, he was, literally, the boy next door. Their mothers were on twelve charitable committees together and did lunch twice a week. Their fathers played golf and did business together. She'd spent her whole life hearing about how great Connor was. Sometimes it was like their entire social circle existed merely to live in the shadow of his greatness. They were the same age, went to the same prep school, had many of the same friends, and folks had been pushing them at each other since puberty.

It didn't seem to matter to anyone that they didn't like each other, and that Connor went out of his way to annoy her whenever possible.

People were shallow. They let good looks and talent outweigh deep personality flaws.

Or else she was just the lucky recipient of whatever the reverse of charm was. Connor didn't care about much beyond his own universe—which he was the center of, of course—so it irked her no end that he'd been chosen this year to colead the fundraising drive. This was supposed to be about other people, but now it would be all about him.

Losing the Saints and Sinners competition would suck regardless, but losing to Connor would just be more than her pride could stand.

And pride was all that was keeping her in her seat at the moment. She'd need to draw on that pride to save her in the coming weeks.

Conscientious eating kept her from having to make any kind of conversation, and she used the time to mentally flip through her Rolodex and plan out new strategies. She needed to think big—beyond just New Orleans. That would be tough, though, for most of the world had forgotten about the city once the Katrina news left the spotlight.

She could involve her sorority for sure. Maybe she could go to the national level. Hell, she needed to get the whole Greek Council involved. All of her pageant connections, up to and including that former Miss Indiana, every favor she was owed was going to have to be called in. She needed to get creative, since all Connor had to do was smile and the money and the votes would pile up.

Ugh. She'd spent weeks looking forward to this, hugging the secret to herself and looking forward to everything Saints and Sinners entailed. But now... All the joy and excitement had been sucked out of it. Her heart sank as she accepted the reality that, despite her efforts, she was probably going to lose through no fault of her own. That brief moment onstage when she'd congratulated herself for the accomplishment felt foolish now. They'd probably just picked her to add contrast and interest to Connor's selection. She hated Connor just a little more.

No. She gave herself a strong mental shake. She would *not* let Connor take that from her. She'd *earned* this title.

And, while she might lose the competition, by God she was going to make it as close as possible. At least she'd keep her dignity and gain satisfaction for a job well done for a good cause.

Dignity. Hmm... How *was* she going to keep her dignity through all of this?

A wicked idea pinged and the more she thought about it, the better it sounded.

She couldn't control Connor or the contest, but she *could* control herself. She'd been chosen to be the Saint. She just needed to be saintly and gracious. In contrast, Connor would look like an arrogant schmuck *and* go slowly insane at the same time. It would be a small victory, but she'd take it nonetheless.

She set her fork down carefully and reached for her wineglass. "Connor?"

"Yes, Vivi?"

She raised the glass in a toast, and Connor's look turned wary. "To a good competitor and a good cause. I'm looking forward to the adventure, because the real winners are the people and the communities we're going to help. I'm glad you came home to be a part of it."

Connor's eyebrows disappeared into his hairline in his shock, but he recovered quickly and picked up his glass. As he touched it to hers she heard a rumble skitter over the crowd, and there was a strobe of flashes. She put on her very best I'm-so-happy-to-be-first-runner-up smile.

The look that crossed Connor's face made it all worthwhile. This might be fun after all.

It was certainly going to be satisfying.

TWO

—

It was well after midnight by the time Vivi made it home. The clubs on Frenchman Street were going strong, and though it was January, the nights were mild enough that a sweatshirt provided enough warmth. All the tables on the sidewalks were packed. In some places the crowds spilled out into the street, and she had to slow almost to a crawl to avoid pedestrians the last few blocks before turning into her driveway. She'd grown up on the tree-lined quiet streets of the Garden District, so adjusting to the much more active nightlife of the Marigny Triangle had been difficult at first, but now she couldn't imagine living anywhere else. Coming home always made her smile.

Sam, her neighbor, was on his porch, drinking a beer and listening to the buskers in Washington Square. He waved and called out, "Congrats, Saint Vivi."

Lorelei had probably spread the news. "Thanks, Sam." She should stop and talk for a few minutes, but she was exhausted, her head was pounding, and her cheeks ached from all the smiling. Plus, the straps from the harness that had held her wings on had chafed against her skin, irritating her almost as much as Connor.

All she wanted to do was wash off the glitter and go to bed. She needed to be up early in the morning to work the phone lines. Another glass of wine was tempting, but sleep would work just as well against the Connor-induced headache.

But, unsurprisingly, Lorelei had waited up for her. They hadn't had much time at the Saints and Sinners Ball to talk beyond quick congratulations.

"There she is," Lorelei sang to a familiar tune. "Saint Vi-vi-enne."

Vivi obligingly did her pageant wave and wiped away an imaginary tear before dropping her purse and bags and sinking onto the couch next to Lorelei with a sigh.

"I can't believe you didn't tell me, Vivi."

"It was top secret stuff. I found out just after Thanksgiving, so I'd have time to make the necessary arrangements to my schedule. It's going to be really busy between now and Mardi Gras."

"We're all so proud. Mama and Daddy were about to burst with it."

"I noticed. But I hope *you're* rethinking your annual pledge of allegiance to the Sinners now. I'm counting on your support."

Lorelei crinkled her nose. "But the Sinners are much more fun."

"Don't make me play the sister card."

"You sure you want me? Your halo might be tarnished by association."

"Repent, reform and sin no more, my child."

Lorelei snorted. "Don't push your luck. One saint is plenty for the LaBlanc family, and it isn't going to be me. That's your job."

"Yep." They'd had similar conversations before, but for the first time she felt a small stab of envy for Lorelei's freedom before she stomped it down. Adopting a bit of Lorelei's attitude might make the next few weeks easier. She kicked off her shoes and leaned back. "Okay, just aim for temporary sainthood. A couple of weeks won't kill you."

"But it will still be painful..." Lorelei wrinkled her nose again. She liked to play the bad girl too much for comfort, but somehow it worked for her. "You know, no one has ever considered me saint-like in any way. It will be a challenge." Lorelei squared her shoulders. "And LaBlancs love a challenge."

"Amen."

"Speaking of challenges..." Lorelei started, and Vivi knew what was coming next "...you did quite well not ripping Connor's head off at the ball."

Vivi felt herself snarl. "I totally understand the choice—it's great PR, money will come rolling in, blah, blah, blah—but, *yeesh*. Is there wine?"

"I'll pour." Lorelei disappeared into the kitchen and returned with two glasses. "I have to agree that it's *brilliant* PR, but you need to be careful."

"I promise it will be justifiable homicide. I won't ask you to bail me out of jail."

Lorelei leveled a look at her. "Do I really need to bring up your coronation ball?"

"No. I've already had those flashbacks tonight."

"Good. Remember you don't want to look bad, so *you're* the one who's going to have to be gracious."

Vivi raised her glass in a mock toast. "Luckily I came to that conclusion on my own earlier."

"*That* explains your good behavior." Lorelei returned the toast. "Good for you, Vivi. You're growing as a person."

Vivi snorted into her glass and earned a suspicious look from Lorelei. "Vivienne LaBlanc, what did you do?"

The smile was hard to fight, but Vivi would stick to the truth regardless. "Nothing. Nothing at all."

The suspicious look sharpened. "*What* did you do?"

"I was gracious, kind and friendly. Perfectly saint-like."

"Exactly the actions that will make Connor wonder if you poisoned his meal."

Vivi bit back the laugh and shrugged instead. "I can't control Connor's thoughts or behavior. If he wants to look foolish and juvenile, he'll have to go there alone."

"You know that *I* find you two endlessly entertaining, but honestly, Vivi—"

She held up a hand. "Lorelei, don't start. Why do we have to go through this every single time Connor's name is mentioned?"

"Because it's just ridiculous. I like Connor—"

"I know. You started his fan club."

A pink flush climbed up her neck. "Someone had to."

"Three years before his first record came out?"

Lorelei tried to brush it off. "He's a nice guy, you know."

"You barely know him."

"I know enough. I know he's had some bad PR recently—"

Vivi nearly choked. "*Bad PR?* Good Lord, Lorelei, the man's fresh off a scandal that covered the tabloids for weeks."

"The DNA tests cleared him of paternity."

"That only means he wasn't the father and escaped child support. The rest..."

"You're taking the tabloids at face value? I can't believe that. You're always telling me not to jump to judgment of people based on rumors."

"No one is rushing to judgment. I'm just saying that you don't really know him—at least not now that he's an adult. And you know *nothing* of his sex life beyond chatter in the high school bathrooms. Who knows what he's really into?"

Lorelei shook her head. "I don't believe Connor could change that much."

"He lives a life we can't even begin to imagine."

"Still, I stand by my earlier assertion that he's a good guy."

Vivi shook her head. "I had no idea you could be swayed by good looks alone."

That earned her a cheeky smile. "At least you admit he's good-looking."

"I'm not blind. I just know that a pretty face can hide an evil heart."

"Another scar from your pageant battles, Vivi?"

One of many. "Oh, hush. I'm not saying Connor's a serial killer in his spare time. *I* just don't like him."

"Then tell me why." Expectation written all over her

face, Lorelei leaned back into the corner of the couch and stared at her. "And I mean it. No wiggling out."

Vivi struggled for words. She was really too fried to handle deep conversations tonight. Charm and personality were like superpowers, and both Lorelei and Connor had them in spades. Connor, though, had turned supervillain with his, and used those powers for evil instead of good. Lorelei had never used her superpowers against Vivi or anyone else to get something she wanted. Lorelei didn't use people the way Connor did. So it probably made it hard for her to see how someone else could.

Vivi sighed because it was just too hard to put into words. "Are you trying to tell me that you've never met a single person that you didn't like? Who just rubbed you the wrong way?"

"Of course I have, but I'm not you. You like everyone. Everyone likes you. You're the closest thing I've ever seen remotely close to an actual saint, so this irrational and extremely juvenile head-butting with Connor just isn't you. It doesn't make sense." Her blue eyes narrowed and sisterly concern crept into her voice. "Is there something you're not telling me? Did Connor...?"

I do not need that kind of rumor floating around. "No. There's nothing dark or evil lurking."

"There were all those rumors around the time you were Mississippi River Princess..."

"And they nearly cost me the crown. But none of them were remotely true."

She saw Lorelei wasn't totally convinced. Funny that she'd never mentioned those rumors bothered her before now.

"You swear?"

"Hand to God."

"Good. Because I *will* kill him for you if I need to."

The show of loyalty warmed her. At least Lorelei liked her better than she liked Connor. "Thank you, sweetie, but it's not necessary. If Connor needed killing, I'd have taken care of it already."

That lightened Lorelei's mood. "Then tell me. How bad can it be? Did he pull your hair in kindergarten? Steal your lunch money? Tease you?"

"Yes." Lorelei frowned and Vivi shrugged. "He did sing that song he wrote about me all the way to Baton Rouge on the eighth-grade field trip."

"Oh, well, that explains it all." Lorelei snorted. "Connor Mansfield wrote you a *song*. No wonder you hate him so much."

"It was called 'Vivi in a Tizzy.'"

Lorelei raised an eyebrow. "I love you, *cherie*, but you often were."

"That's beside the point. No fourteen-year-old girl wants a cute fourteen-year-old boy making fun of her."

"Ah, I see. There's a little unrequited tween crush—"

Oh, for a different choice of words. "Stop right there." Lorelei grinned at her.

"First of all, I happen to know for a fact that you failed Psych 101, so please don't try to analyze me. Secondly, we don't live in a sitcom. And third, I'm really, really tired of people shoving Connor in my face and telling me to like him. That's just annoying and it makes me like him even less."

"That's hardly his fault."

Maybe it was the wine, the late hour or just the exhaustion, but Vivi finally sighed. "Marie Lester."

Lorelei looked confused until she placed the name. "What's Marie got to do with it?"

"He used me to get to her."

"What?"

Vivi rubbed a hand over her face. *This* was why she didn't want to talk about it. "You know how sheltered and sweet Marie was, right?" At Lorelei's nod, she continued, "That's why her parents sent her to St. Katharine's. New Orleans is this big bad sin city, and they figured she'd be safe there."

"And?"

"Junior year, Connor's friend Reg asked Marie out and she said no. She considered them a bunch of hellraisers, and she was too good for that. Connor took that as some kind of challenge and a chance to show up Reg."

"Okay...but still not really following you."

She took a big gulp of wine. "Well, Marie and I were lab partners and her parents just loved me, you know."

"Of course."

"So Connor started hanging around me, being nice and all, in order to make himself look better to Marie."

Lorelei nodded. "Because if *you* said he was an okay guy then Marie might change her mind?"

"Exactly."

"So *that's* why Connor started hanging around our house more."

"He was just using me to get to her. And to top it all off he didn't really like her. He just wanted to prove *he* could get Marie when his friend had failed."

"It's a jerk move, but really..." Vivi shot a look at her and Lorelei trailed off. "Oh. You thought he was interested in you. Ouch. *That's* why you slapped him at your coronation."

The hurt and humiliation she'd felt at seventeen might have been dulled by time, but her twenty-eight-year-old self remembered the blow to her ego and pride. She nodded.

Lorelei rolled her eyes. "That was years ago. Teenage crap. I don't know a nice way to say this, but...get over it."

"He lied to me, used me, hurt me and made me an unwilling accomplice in his quest to use Marie in order to one-up one of his friends. I don't care if it *was* teenage crap. He was wrong. And, even worse, I should have known better. Even after years of his crap I fell for it."

"And you can't just let it go?" Lorelei shook her head. "Wow, Vivi. That's *really* mature."

"This from the girl who is still mad at Steve Milner for cheating on her."

"He left me at prom to go have sex with another girl!"

"So call me when you're over that and we'll talk again about teenage crap I need to get over."

Lorelei's lips pressed into a thin line. Vivi had made her point.

"Even if I wanted to let that slide, I haven't really seen anything in the intervening years to convince me that Connor isn't still an arrogant, self-centered man-child. If anything, his fame has only fueled it. And since Connor is still holding on to his preadolescent grudges against *me,* I'm not too worried about maturity."

It was Lorelei's turn to rub her eyes. "I think I need more wine for this to make any sense at all."

Vivi patted her sister's knee. "Look at it from a different perspective. Animosity will add interest to the competition. If Connor and I suddenly bury the hatchet and become best buddies, people will be disappointed. And I'd hate to deny Bon Argent the opportunity to exploit this for a good cause's gain."

Lorelei sighed. "I hate it when the words you say *sound* perfectly reasonable even though it's actually crazy talk. How do you even manage that?"

"It's a gift." Vivi looked down and noticed she was shedding glitter on the sofa cushions. The glitter reminded her of her purpose, and her personal problems with Connor weren't it. "So you've got my back? I need all the help I can get."

Lorelei nodded. "Blood—however crazy that blood is—is thicker than water, so I'll be as saintly as possible for the duration of your reign. I await my marching orders."

"Good." Vivi grabbed one of the bags and dug inside for a T-shirt. "Welcome to Team Saint."

Lorelei unfolded the powder-blue shirt and scowled at the angel wings emblazoned across the back. "Do I really have to wear this?"

"Yep. Every minute you can. And your first assignment is Tuesday. We're going to the lower Ninth Ward for cleanup detail."

The scowl morphed into horror. "I didn't realize you meant for me to do manual labor."

"It's good for the soul, honey, if bad for your manicure."

"I think I might have to work on Tuesday," she grumbled.

"*I* think it's safe to assume that Daddy will give you the time off."

"Fine." Lorelei looked at the shirt again, distaste written across her face. "This is *not* in my color palette. What color are the shirts for Connor's team?"

"Don't even joke about that. I'm already at a great disadvantage without my sister defecting to the dark side."

"Okay, here's the thing, Vivi. It's ridiculous, but I'll back off. However, I'm not going to listen to you moan about Connor for the next four weeks. It'll ruin my whole Mardi Gras."

Vivi just wished someone had taken that into consideration before they'd stuck her with Connor for the next month. The rest of the city may be planning on *laissez le bons temps rouler,* but her *temps* weren't looking very *bon* at the moment.

Connor spent most of Sunday morning and part of the afternoon on the phone with his manager and his agent, but the chore didn't aggravate him as much when he could sit on a balcony overlooking Royal Street with a *café au lait* and real beignets. The third-floor apartment had been sitting empty while Gabe was in Italy, and Connor appreciated the solitude it offered while still being in the heart of the French Quarter. The street musician below his balcony displayed more enthusiasm than talent, but it was as much a sound of home as the *clop-clop* and jingle of the mule-drawn carriages and the shouts of the tour guides leading groups down the street.

Sitting here in the winter sunshine, his feet propped up on the wrought-iron rail with nothing to do except let his mind wander...bliss. Until this moment he hadn't realized how stressed he'd been.

Even the doctor's orders to rest his hands and wrists seemed less onerous and restrictive today. The piano wasn't calling him, and the only workout his hands were getting involved lifting his coffee cup to his mouth repeatedly. Even after hours on the phone his head felt clear, and he could feel his muscles relaxing and the pain receding—no pharmaceutical intervention necessary.

Yep, bliss. He might just sit here all day and attempt absolutely nothing more strenuous than a solid nap.

His mother was a bit irritated that he'd chosen to stay in a friend's apartment instead of his childhood home, but this was a high-profile visit, and he didn't want photographers or fans staking out his parents' house and trampling Mom's flowers. This was just easier.

He wasn't the only celebrity to call New Orleans home, but coming straight off tour to the Saints and Sinners fundraiser right after Katy Arras and her accusations... It was best to let that all die down some first.

People would be used to having him around again soon enough, and in time, it would no longer be big news.

God, he loved this city.

Which was why he'd jumped at the chance to be this

year's Sinner. Silliness aside, it was an honor, and he felt very much the hometown boy made good. He was glad his fame guaranteed big money this year for the fundraiser, even if it created an "uneven playing field" that steamed Vivi's oysters.

Speaking of Vivi...

The view from Gabe's apartment balcony contained a surprise: he had a clear view to the front door to Vivi's art gallery just a few buildings up Royal. According to Mom, who kept him fully up-to-date on all of the goings-on in New Orleans—*especially* those of her friends and their children—Vivi's gallery was doing very well, walking the line between art that was accessible and sellable yet still high-end quality.

Good for Vivi. He'd had no clue that art was Vivi's passion, but after years of hearing all about her pageant successes—Good Lord, her reign as Miss Louisiana had been one of the longest years of his life—it was good to know that she could do something other than twirl batons and look pretty. She'd always had brains; it was nice to know she'd finally decided to use them for something.

Thanks to Mom, he also knew that Vivi wasn't a surprise choice for Saint at all. If the city could canonize her they probably would. Vivi was involved in *everything;* any organization that needed a face or a volunteer had Vivi on speed dial. The only surprise was that they hadn't made her the Saint long before now. Cynically, he wondered if Max and the board had held off until his schedule had cleared so they could get the maximum impact.

The morning paper had been almost gleeful about

the announcement, making sure to illustrate their "antagonistic relationship" with anecdotes that dated all the way back to their seventh-grade performance of *Bye Bye Birdie,* just in case there were people in town who *weren't* aware that the children of two of the city's oldest and most influential families were at odds like an alternate universe's Romeo and Juliet.

For years he'd held out hope that everyone would move on, but it just went to show that no matter how big he got, or how many millions of records he sold, people would never let anyone live down their past. Especially if that past was something they could still milk for attention and laughs.

But it was his time to milk the cash cow he'd become. Half-formed ideas that had been swimming in his mind were getting even more solid, and the pieces were falling into place with a rapidity that felt like fate intervening. The old coffee warehouse on Julia Street, investors like Gabe lining up with their wallets open...

If this all worked out—and it was looking like it just might—he'd be more than just a hometown boy done good. He'd be a part of this town in a way he'd never planned on before. Some of this was very new territory for him, but it felt good. It felt right. He didn't have to put down roots here; the roots were here, waiting for him to come back. He just had to make sure they didn't strangle him this time.

Mom might have thought his desire to be a musician was an act of defiance—a revolt against the expectations of going to college, joining Dad's firm, marrying a nice local girl like one of the LaBlancs, and settling down in a mansion three blocks away. In retrospect, she might have been a little right, but other than the occasional unpleasant run through the tabloids and the time away from home she really couldn't complain. Well, she was still pushing the nice-girl-big-house-some-grandkids agenda...

Which, oddly, brought him back to Vivi.

If he was serious about spending more time here at home he'd have to call some kind of truce with Vivi. Come to some kind of understanding. The circles they ran in overlapped occasionally, thanks to their parents and shared friends. They wouldn't be able to completely avoid or ignore each other.

Fame had its privileges, but Vivi had clout. People respected her, and her opinions went a long way. It would be hard to claim he was trying to do something good if Vivi objected. Hell, you couldn't even claim to be a decent human being in this town if Vivi hated you. People might like him for various reasons, but everyone *loved* Vivi and courted her approval. As long as she hated him, folks would wonder why. And they'd assume it was all his fault.

God, it was annoying.

And while Vivi had miraculously become the most gracious and polite dinner partner he'd ever had Friday night, he doubted that graciousness would continue once she found out he was planning a return to what she no doubt considered *her* turf now.

Vivi would be fit to be tied, and he almost looked forward to telling her. *No,* he thought, walking that thought back in light of his earlier conclusions. He didn't need her approval—though it would help—but he did need her tolerance. Egging her on wouldn't help his cause.

He hadn't fully realized that he'd been staring at the door to Vivi's gallery until the door opened and Vivi stepped outside. He started to slide back, but then realized she had no reason to look up, and probably wouldn't see him even if she happened to do so. She paused mid-step, digging through her bag and pulling out a phone.

Two men standing next to a car gawked openly at Vivi, and realistically he couldn't blame them. The black pencil skirt emphasized her legs and tiny waist, and the upswept hair showcased the line of her neck and high cheekbones. One of the men seemed to be encouraging the other to go over and speak to her. *She is way out of your league, buddy,* Connor thought. Vivi was, to quote his departed grandmother, "a prime example of good breeding and a proper upbringing."

She finished her call and set a pair of sunglasses on her face before walking briskly toward the corner and turning on to St. Ann's Street toward Jackson Square. Connor—and most of the other men on the street—watched her until she was out of sight.

Tomorrow he and Vivi would start the morning show media blitz, hitting all the local TV stations and kicking off the fundraising in earnest. After that, it was breakfast with some big donors and organization heads and a photo call. Most of his day would be spent in Vivi's company.

While she'd been polite and gracious the other night, Connor didn't believe for a second that it wasn't an act. He knew her too well to fall for that. She was out to prove something by *not* sniping at him. He wouldn't try to guess what her overall goal was—beyond not making herself look bad in the press—but he would not help her achieve it by attacking first. It played right into his plans to have her publically playing nice. It gave him her stamp of approval without her actually giving it. She probably hadn't thought that part through. Talk about steaming her oysters.

He might be the Sinner—and it might be a well-deserved title—but Vivi wasn't the only one who knew how to behave.

It would be interesting to see who broke first.

THREE

—

The reporter with the plastic smile thought she was being very clever, but Vivi knew what was coming. Intentionally trying to fluster a guest with "gotcha" questions was unbelievably rude, in her opinion, but it was standard fare and just part of the game.

If Chatty Cathy here thinks she can fluster me, though, that girl is in for a big surprise.

She'd had every derogatory stereotype about pageants thrown in her face by reporters with more gravitas and bigger audiences and hadn't broken. It might have been a few years, but she hadn't forgotten how this was done. A couple of comments and questions about Connor weren't going to tie her tongue and cause her to say something stupid. Or scandalously quotable out of context.

The smile grew wider. *Bring it,* Vivi thought, and let her own smile widen a bit, too.

"So, Vivienne, how did you feel when Connor's name was announced Friday night? Were you very shocked?"

Vivi nodded, and the reporter brightened a bit, obviously figuring she'd hit the mark. *Amateur.* "Just as much as everyone else, I imagine. With Connor's career taking off like it has, I never dreamed his schedule would allow him to come back and do something like Saints and Sinners."

"So no problems, then, with this matchup?"

"Sort of." She waited just long enough to tease that there might be a sound bite forthcoming. "I am quite competitive, and I wish they'd chosen someone who'd be easier to beat. But then I remind myself that, while this *is* a competition, there are no real losers in it. The money raised through Saints and Sinners does so much good for the community, and everyone involved is a winner."

Answer the question, but deflect the intent and bring the interview back to the proper topic.

"And what about you, Connor?"

Vivi kept her face neutral as she turned toward him and thought, *Don't screw this up now.* Surely Connor's fame meant he had the experience to answer this? She thought of a dozen good answers and tried to think them hard enough that Connor might pick one up through ESP.

"I was pretty shocked myself to be chosen this year, but it's an honor that actually brings with it the chance to do something good for a lot of people. So, like Vivi said, we all win—although I do hope to put on a good show at least." He shot the lady-killer grin at the reporter, and now that he'd shaved off the goatee, his dimple was clearly visible. When he added a wink, the reporter blushed slightly and fumbled over her next words.

Oh, good Lord. Spare me the simpering females. Women had been falling all over themselves since Connor hit puberty, but the maturation of his features and body combined with his fame and charm... Vivi might understand the reaction, but she was still ashamed of her entire gender.

But she had to admit that Connor had done well dodging the impertinent question.

Unable to get a good answer out of Connor, the reporter had no choice but to cut to the graphic listing the upcoming events and direct people to the Saints and Sinners website. The camera turned to the station's meteorologist for the weather report and Vivi unhooked her mic.

Making all four local morning shows in two hours meant that their schedule was very tight, and there was no time to waste in idle chitchat. Connor, however, had decided to stop to sign autographs and pose for pictures. Vivi bit her tongue and waited with what she hoped looked like patience.

Finally, though, she had to step in and break up the love-fest. "I'm so sorry, y'all, but we're going to be late for our next interview if we don't leave right now."

Connor fell into step beside her as they exited the building. "Thanks for the save. It's hard to get away sometimes."

"You can't do that at every stop this morning or we'll never make them all. I know you just hate to tear yourself away, but there are other people's schedules to consider."

"And *there's* the mood swing to the Vivi I know." He sighed dramatically. "I knew that perkiness was too good to last."

Damn it, she'd already forgotten her pledge to be gracious and polite. "It's six o'clock in the morning. I need to save all my perkiness for the cameras. Sorry."

The driver had fresh coffee from a nearby shop waiting for them in the car. She nearly hugged him in gratitude—both for the caffeine and the chance to gather her thoughts and adjust her tone as she took a few sips and settled in.

"However, I don't have the skill set necessary to be your bouncer, so you'll need to either provide one yourself or else learn how to extract yourself from the fawning adulation of your fans."

Connor leveled a look at her across the backseat. "Without those people I have no career. They support me. So the least I can do for them is sign an autograph and smile for the camera. Mock me all you like, but don't *ever* mock my fans."

The words were hard and cold, and that combination got her attention. She'd never heard Connor speak like that. "You're actually serious."

"As a heart attack."

Vivi felt about two feet tall. "My apologies, then, for insulting your fans."

Connor nodded his acceptance of her apology, then pulled his phone out of his pocket and began to tap at it. Vivi was glad for his distraction; she needed a moment to process. She'd seen Connor's posing and autographing as glory-mongering—something to feed his ego. She hadn't expected Connor to get so passionate about it. It made sense, though. He *wouldn't* have a career without fans, so he should be apprecia-tive of them.

She just wouldn't have guessed that he would be.

Connor didn't look up from his phone. "By the way, good job deflecting that question and refram-ing. You've had media training."

The terminology gave him away. "As have you, it seems."

"I learned the hard way that performing onstage and doing an interview are two totally different things. I only had to screw up once before I swore I'd never make that mistake again. What made you do it?"

Was he being intentionally dense? "About the time I won Mississippi River Princess I realized I really needed it." She paused, but Connor didn't make the connection. "I had my sights on Miss Louisiana and Miss America. I had a platform to promote, a title to represent and a reputation to protect. There was no way I was going in unprepared for the job."

"I hadn't thought about that. It doesn't really look like that hard of a job."

She snorted. "I could say the same thing about your job, you know."

He looked at her like she was insane. "*You've* never done a six-month world tour."

"And *you've* never been Miss Louisiana."

"It's not all glory and encores, you know. It's hard, exhausting, cutthroat work."

She smiled sweetly at him. "So is the Miss Amer-ica pageant."

Connor's eyes widened at the implication. "I'm just

surprised there's more to it than showing up and looking pretty."

"Somehow your lack of insight doesn't really surprise me."

"No need to get so huffy about it."

She caught herself mid-huff and lifted her chin instead. "I really don't have the patience to school you
on incorrect pageant stereotypes this morning. If you
want to believe I'm nothing more than an airhead,
so be it. I've been called worse by better. But just let
me remind you that my reign was over years ago. My
tiara-wearing days are behind me, and I've moved on
to other things to be proud of."

"Like your gallery?"

"Yes." She was very proud of the gallery and happy
to brag about it to anyone who would listen—including Connor. And it seemed like a safe enough topic. "It
seemed to take forever to get off the ground, but it's
doing really well now. We've recently been able to offer
patronage to a few young emerging artists—provid-
ing studio space and a small stipend."

"Good for you, Vivi."

She couldn't tell if that was sarcasm or not. Not that
she would bite back—she was determined to keep a
better hold of her tongue if it killed her—but she'd
still like to know if Connor was mocking her. His face
was inscrutable as he leaned back against the leather
seats of the limo and closed his eyes.

"Wake me when we get there."

And now I'm an alarm clock? Connor was obviously
used to traveling with an entourage to cater to him.
Don't be so touchy. If it were anyone other than Connor,

she knew it wouldn't bother her quite as much. Still, though…it was rude to decide to nap instead of make polite conversation. Not that she *wanted* to make polite conversation, but it was the principle of the thing.

Connor stretched out his long legs, taking up a bit more than his fair share of the available space, and crossed his feet at the ankles. Amazingly, he seemed to be asleep a second later, his breathing slow and deep. *How did he do that?*

But that left her crawling through morning traffic in the back of a town car with no one to talk to. She could lower the privacy screen and talk to the driver, but thanks to Connor hogging the space she'd have to contort herself in order to accomplish that.

She pulled out her phone instead, to check her mail, but her eyes drifted to the big black boots parked next to her simple black flats. *Big feet,* she thought, *to match his big head.*

The head in question was tipped back against the headrest. Shaving the goatee really did make a difference, making his mouth seem more prominent and emphasizing that strong chin. Even with his features relaxed in sleep, Connor projected attitude.

He might be a piano-playing crooner, but Connor *looked* the part of a bad-boy rock star, and that image had helped fuel his popularity. Women loved the idea of a man who looked like *that* singing love songs in a voice that could send shivers all the way down to their toes. He was practically a musical fantasy come to life.

Even she had to admit—privately, of course—that Connor was freakin' gorgeous. Broad shoulders, lean hips, a smile that caused feminine flusters every single time... A woman would have to be blind or dead not to appreciate him based on looks alone, and she was neither. She wasn't ignorant or denying of his attributes; she was just immune to them because she knew him.

Wow, it was getting hot in here. The man radiated heat like a generator. Vivi had to fan herself. She did *not* want to go on TV all sweaty and red-faced. The climate controls were next to Connor, out of her reach unless she wanted to crawl across his lap, so she'd settle for cracking a window for fresh air.

The windows on her side of the car didn't seem to open, so that meant she'd have to open the ones on the other side. But Connor's legs blocked easy access to those controls, too. *Who designed this vehicle?* She should just wake him up, but that would seem petty and she was *not* going to be petty.

At least outwardly. *Inwardly* was a different situation.

Vivi slid to the edge of the seat, pushed up, placed one knee in her seat and lifted the other leg over Connor's. She was reaching for the handle on the other side to pull herself over without touching him when the driver braked hard, jerking her forward and then backward as the car came to a stop.

Vivi lost her balance and fell back, landing hard and ungracefully in Connor's lap.

Connor had merely been dozing, but the sudden stop of the car jerked him awake a split second before Vivi landed in his lap.

His arms went around her instinctively to steady her as she slid sideways, and his first ridiculous thought was that Vivi was a nice armful. She was small, but compact: the butt pressed against his groin was firm, and the thigh under his hand lean and strong. The curves he'd admired the other day felt even better than they looked. His body tightened and his skin heated at the contact.

Vivi's head was just below his shoulder, and the light floral scent that always faintly surrounded her filled his lungs as he inhaled. He could feel her heartbeat and realized that his *other* hand had landed directly on her breast; the soft curve filled his palm perfectly. Something flashed through him, landing in his lap with as much force as Vivi had.

He moved his hand away, brushing her hair out of her face instead. "You okay?" he asked as he uncovered her mouth.

"I'm fine." She scrambled to an upright position and scooted off his lap into the seat beside him and began finger-combing her hair back into place.

The privacy screen slid open and the driver's concerned face appeared. "Sorry about that. Some idiot ran the light. You two okay?"

"I think so," Vivi answered, but her voice was a little shaky. "Connor?"

"Fine," he answered. While it seemed like Vivi had been in his lap for a long time, he realized only a few seconds had actually passed. Still, though, his body had reacted like a horny teenager's, as if he'd never touched a girl before.

This was *Vivi*, for God's sake.

He shifted in the seat, trying to find a more comfortable position while he got it back under control.

Vivi's face was flushed, and he noticed her hands were shaking the tiniest bit. "Are you sure you're okay?"

"I'm fine, really." As the car started forward again Vivi moved to the other seat. "I was trying to get across to open the window when we stopped. Sorry I landed on you."

Maybe it *was* a little warm in here. He jumped on the excuse and pushed the button to lower the window. Fresh air filled the car, dispersing both the heat and the tension in the air. "Better?"

"Much."

Vivi swallowed hard, and when she lifted her eyes to meet his and smile her thanks, he noticed how wide they were. How the pupils had dilated until the blue was a thin circle. Color still flagged her cheeks, and her breath had a ragged edge.

Vivi couldn't hold the look or the smile, and she began to dig in her bag, emerging with lipstick and a mirror. Her hands still weren't steady, and she concentrated on the task like it was the most important thing she'd ever done.

He hadn't been the only one affected by those few seconds, and it looked like Vivi was still riding the shockwave. *That* knowledge slammed into him, and the air felt warm again.

"Oh, look—we're here." Vivi spoke rapidly, with relief dripping off her words, and she had the door open before the car came to a complete stop in front of the studio. "I'm going to run in and freshen up real quick before we go on air." Then she bolted for the building like the hounds of hell were on her heels.

Honestly, he didn't blame her at all.

* * *

Vivi needed to splash cold water on her face, but that would only make her mascara run and then she'd look like a raccoon during the interview. She settled for wetting a paper towel and running it over her neck and under the collar of her shirt to cool her skin.

Checking under the stall doors for feet and seeing none, Vivi let her breath out in a deep sigh and braced her hands on the counter.

Sweet mercy.

I was in his lap.

And his hand was...

And the other was...

Oh, she knew exactly where each hand had landed. She felt branded from the touch.

His hands weren't the only part of him that had burned into her skin. Her butt had... He'd... *She'd*... Dear heaven, she couldn't have landed in that exact position if she'd tried.

Mortified wasn't a strong enough word.

Maybe if she hadn't been ogling him just seconds before she might not now feel like she'd intentionally given him a lap dance.

That was bad enough, but worse was the realization that for a split second she'd enjoyed the embrace.

And so did he, a little voice said. The evidence had been impossible to miss.

But then she'd fluttered and stammered and... *Ugh.* She'd seen that look: he *knew.* And with his ego...

Her quick wish that the floor would open and swallow her went ungranted. Instead she dug for a comb and tried to repair the damage she'd done to her hair with her fingers earlier. After a critical look, she shrugged and let it go at presentable. Hopefully that flush would fade before they went on camera, but considering she was going to have to face Connor, she'd probably look like a ripe tomato all through the interview.

Connor was a hottie, but she was immune. She was not so shallow as to allow good looks and an amazing body sway her. She liked men with substance.

Somebody tell that to my libido.

"Vivienne?" A young woman poked her head around the door. "If you're ready, we really need to get you miked."

"Coming." Vivi checked her teeth for lipstick in a last-ditch stall for time, but she really had no choice but to follow the woman out into the hallway.

Connor stood about twenty feet away by the studio door, autographing a CD case. He handed it and the pen back to the waiting fan, then smiled as a third person snapped a photo. He looked up as the woman shooed the other two away. His eyes met Vivi's briefly before he looked away.

Great. Now I can add uncomfortable sexual tension to this nightmare. And while Connor had plenty of fans who wanted to meet him, talk to him, get his autograph or generally just slobber all over him, she didn't have anything or anyone to distract *her.* She had no choice but to stand there feeling foolish as Connor charmed and dazzled them all.

It might not be so bad if she hadn't just realized— even if only for a second—that she was just as prone to simpering and flustering as the women basking in his charm right now.

No, that was embarrassing, and knowledge she wished she didn't have, but that wasn't completely it. Facing that unhappy truth just seemed to open the gate to other, far more disturbing truths.

Mainly that Connor's life was taking off and hers had already plateaued.

Art galleries in New Orleans weren't nearly as interesting as concert tours and celebrity-studded parties in Los Angeles. She'd done dozens of interviews at this station before, but all for various charities, and everyone knew her story already.

Connor was exciting and interesting and she felt every bit the washed-up beauty queen whose fifteen minutes were over. At twenty-eight she'd already peaked, and was now just another socialite doing the rounds and clinging to past glory.

Depression hit like a brick.

She didn't begrudge Connor his success or his popularity—even she would admit that he was extremely talented—but it still forced her to admit that Connor had something she didn't: the "It" factor. Nothing really set her apart. She was just average.

Average wasn't bad, but being stuck next to someone so obviously above average was more damaging to her ego than she'd expected. Was this new simpering and flustered reaction to Connor a symptom of a larger issue?

Was she really that shallow?

* * *

Something was off. Vivi answered all the questions, shook all the hands and smiled for the cameras appropriately, but *something* wasn't right. Connor couldn't put his finger on exactly what, but he had no doubt that Vivi had something on her mind.

He was hardly an expert on Vivi's moods, but she lacked her normal sparkle—or at least the sparkle she normally gave off to other people. People who weren't him.

When she did speak to him directly—which wasn't often and lessened to almost complete silence as the day continued—her voice lacked that normal Vivi edge. Her answers bordered on a monotone, and she passed up several easy opportunities to mock him outright.

He'd been looking for ways to broker some kind of peace, but this wasn't at all how he imagined that peace would be.

It was just plain odd. Disturbing, even.

After several hours of this uncomfortable non-conversation—plus a few strange, indefinable looks from Vivi—they were finally done and the driver was taking them home. Vivi spent her time playing with her phone or staring out the window as if she'd never seen the city before.

He'd had a hard time pulling himself back under control after...after whatever it was that had happened earlier. Coupled with her dramatic attitude change, he began to wonder if he'd misread the look on her face. Maybe that hadn't been shock. Horror? Disgust? Offense? Give Vivi the choice of landing in his lap or a slime pit and she'd probably ask if there was any difference.

No, he knew his strengths and weaknesses, and he hadn't misread that look. He'd seen it plenty before. Vivi might have been horrified, but it wasn't necessarily because she'd landed on him. Or that he'd accidentally copped a feel.

Damn. He shouldn't have gone there. The palms of his hands burned with the memory and now he needed a cold shower to offset the effects of it.

Vivi cleared her throat. "About earlier...I was serious."

Connor's train of thought derailed. Surely Vivi wasn't—?

"This is a competition, but we should focus on what's really important."

Oh. He gave himself a good mental shake. "Agreed."

She slid her finger over her phone, looking at something. "You're already kicking my butt with online donations to your war chest, but I still plan to put on a good showing—in the competitions, if nothing else."

"Because that's what's important."

"Of course. You're going to bring in buckets of money and—"

Enough. "I'll match yours." The words were out before he'd even thought them through.

Vivi chuckled. "Oh, you'll surpass mine. I've accepted that."

"No. I mean I'll match yours. Dollar for dollar, whatever you raise, I'll match."

That got her attention and she finally met his eyes. "You can't."

"Worried about my finances?"

"Oh, I don't doubt you can afford it. It's just that any money donated personally by the Sinner and the Saint doesn't go into the final tally."

He relaxed back into his seat and got comfortable. This might be interesting. Could her personal dislike of him outweigh her competitive spirit? His money had never brought him quite so much pleasure before. "I can't count personal donations into my own war chest, but there's nothing in the rules that says I can't donate to yours."

"But why would you?" Vivi was too competitive to even contemplate the idea.

"It levels that playing field."

Vivi's eyes narrowed suspiciously. "What if that puts me over the top?"

"Then you win."

That brought another chuckle, only this time there was real humor behind it. That was progress. "Can your pride handle that, Connor?"

"The question is, can yours?"

She snorted. "Taking your money? Definitely. In fact, it would give me great pleasure."

"There's a first time for everything."

A flush crept up her neck. "As I've said, this isn't about us."

"Then why else would it give you pleasure to beat me?"

"The fact there's a bigger, more important purpose to this competition doesn't preclude me from gaining personal satisfaction."

He raised an eyebrow at her choice of words and

watched the flush get darker. Strangely, it made his pulse kick up a notch.

She cleared her throat. "From beating you, that is. Competition is healthy and good."

"If you say so."

"I do. But I fully expect you to live up to your promise. If you try to renege on this..."

"I always deliver on my promises, Vivi. Always."

A strange silence fell and Vivi looked away. The tension still felt heavy, but it crackled a bit now that pride and challenge had joined it.

The car stopped and Vivi looked out the window, eyebrows drawing together. Reaching for the intercom button, Vivi said, "My car's at my house. I don't know why he came to the gallery."

Connor caught her hand, causing those eyebrows to furrow at him. Then, like his touch was painful, Vivi extracted her hand from his.

"This is *my* stop."

"What?"

"I'm staying in a friend's place."

Vivi looked around. "Where?"

He pointed to Gabe's building.

"But that's Gabe Morrow's building."

"Yeah. He's in Italy right now—"

"I know that. I didn't know *you* knew Gabe, though."

"We have mutual friends. I just didn't know they included you."

"Did you know my gallery is right there?" She pointed.

"I do now. I'd say you were welcome to drop by for a drink sometime..." He let the thought trail off and, predictably, Vivi rolled her eyes. "See you tomorrow, Vivi."

The cool air felt good against his skin as he stepped out of the car, and with Vivi safely away, he began to feel normal again for the first time in hours.

Something had happened today. He just wasn't sure exactly what. Or why. Or how, for that matter. But whatever that *something* was…

Vivi just had the ability to make his brain short-circuit. That was the only explanation.

But while it was nice to have that explanation, it also meant he was going to be permanently brain-damaged by the time this was done.

FOUR

—

It never failed to amaze Vivi how slow recovery was coming to some areas. If not for the tall weeds and faded Xs painted on the buildings, people might think the hurricane had come through weeks ago instead of years. It wasn't something visitors to New Orleans saw unless they specifically came to see it—all the popular tourist areas were up and running—and, unbelievably, it wasn't something *she* saw very often even though she lived in the city. More than distance separated the hardest hit areas like the Lower Ninth Ward from the Garden District and the French Quarter. Less than a third of the residents had been able to return, and the neighborhood felt empty and lifeless. She thought of her own lively neighborhood, and it only made the loss here sharper.

Vivi hauled another bag to the portable Dumpster and grunted as she tossed it in. Her shoulders and arms throbbed and her legs ached, and they'd only been at this for a few hours. There was a big difference between working out at the gym and actually working, and she was feeling it already.

Lorelei appeared beside her, water bottle in hand. Although the day was cool, sweat beaded around her hairline from the work. She had a dirty smudge across one cheek. Like Vivi, she'd layered a thermal shirt under her Team Saint T-shirt, and the sleeves were now dirty and stained.

Lorelei took a long drink and groaned as she leaned against the Dumpster. "You owe me a massage and a manicure."

"Done." The look of surprise on Lorelei's face told Vivi she'd been looking for a chance to grumble, and that look was well worth what she'd pay for the spa. "I do appreciate your help, though. We are kicking Connor's butt."

"It's a fine butt to kick, if you ask me."

"I happen to agree," said Vivi.

Lorelei snorted, and Vivi wanted to suck the words back in.

"It *is* a very fine butt, isn't it? I didn't know you'd noticed."

"Don't you have work to do?"

"Slave-driver." Lorelei pulled her gloves back on. "I feel bad for Connor, though."

"What?"

"It's got to suck to always have a camera following you around. Here he is, trying to do charity work, and while everyone wants him to *talk* about what he's doing, none of them will actually let him *do* it."

Vivi turned to look at the circus on the other side of the street. Connor and his team were being followed by camera crews and reporters. It was good publicity for what they were doing, but it meant Connor's team was doing it very, very slowly. Lorelei had a point, but still... "Pardon me if I don't cry for him."

"Wow, you're mean. It's a good thing the Bon Argent people don't know you better or they'd pull your halo in a heartbeat, Saint Vivi."

"He told me yesterday how much his fans mean to him. He doesn't mind this."

"There's a big difference between fans who love and admire him and the press who just want something from him."

When had Lorelei developed such insights—*and* the need to share them? "Maybe. But the two go hand in hand. He can't have one without the other, so..."

Lorelei patted her on the shoulder. "You just keep clinging to that if it makes you feel better." Grabbing an empty trash bag, she started to walk away. Over her shoulder, though, she tossed one last grenade. "But remember it the next time you wonder why everyone always thought you were so sanctimonious."

Lorelei was too far away for Vivi to rebut the accusation, and her words hung in the air like a rebuke. A very unfair rebuke. She *wasn't* sanctimonious, darn it; she just had a strong inner compass. That wasn't a character flaw; it was practically a virtue. More people needed that kind of inner knowledge; otherwise they ended up in the tabloids like Connor.

But...Connor *was* rather struggling over there, and with the press in the way nothing was going to get done, and that was what was really important. He'd mentioned his loyalty to his fans, but nothing about the press. She could throw him a rope.

Taking a deep breath, she crossed to the middle of the street. Hands on her hips in what she hoped looked like annoyance, she shouted as loud as she could, "Hey, Connor!" Cameras turned in her direction, but she brazened it out. "You gonna stand around all day like a pretty boy or are you gonna work?"

Silence fell. She raised an eyebrow and all the heads swiveled back to Connor for his response. Connor met her eyes and she swore she saw the corner of his mouth twitch into a smile before he caught it.

"It's not that my team doesn't relish kicking your butt," she said, and a cheer went up behind her from her team, "but it just doesn't seem sporting if you're not even trying."

"We're just warming up, Vivi, so don't start celebrating too soon." He turned to the press. "Y'all have enough to run with. You're welcome to stay, but if you do I'm going to expect you to work. I've got some catching up to do."

There were grumbles, both from the media and Connor's team, but the reminder seemed to do the trick. Work gloves were pulled back on, trash bags picked back up and cameras loaded into vans. Connor joined her on the street—neutral territory between the two teams now working in earnest.

Quietly he said, "Thanks. I owe you."

"That's twice now, and I do intend to collect."

"I always pay my debts."

"Good to know. But I should warn you my favors don't come cheap."

"I should certainly hope not." He looked her up and down in a way he never had before, and something fluttery came to life in her stomach. *Damn it, damn it, damn it.* She should be past this kind of juvenile response. But there was just something so raw and sexy about Connor in his black Sinner shirt, jeans and work boots. She'd have to have been dead for a week not to feel the effect. Even with the cameras following him around he'd managed to work up a sweat, and the beads of moisture at his temples only added to that purely masculine vibe.

Focus. "And you won't be getting off quick and easy, either."

"Excellent." Connor obviously found something amusing in this—more amusing than it actually was—and Vivi felt like she was tripping over a current running through the conversation without knowing how or why. "Quick and easy aren't really my style, you know."

What on earth...? Lord, she needed a map to navigate this conversation. "Well, I didn't break that circus up to stand around and chitchat with you, so I think we should both get back to work."

There was that smirk again. "On you go, then."

Vivi stepped back to do just that and immediately tripped over a piece of asphalt knocked loose by the flooding. She landed with a thud, and a sharp pain shot through her left butt cheek. Her eyes watered as she reached under herself and removed another, smaller piece of asphalt. "Ouch."

Connor squatted, amusement and concern written equally on his face. "You okay?"

"Yes." It was embarrassing, but at least the cameras had already been put away. *Small favors.*

"That whole 'grace and poise' thing doesn't actually count as much in the pageant system as we're led to believe, does it?"

"Hush."

There was that grin again. "You're not the first woman to be knocked off-kilter by my presence..."

"Don't flatter yourself."

Conner chuckled and stood. "Should I offer assistance?"

"It would be nice," she snapped.

He extended a hand and hauled her to her feet. Vivi rubbed a hand over the spot where the sharp debris had dug in. "That's going to leave a bruise."

"Want me to rub it for you?"

Shock rocketed through her. "Why don't you just kiss it," she snapped.

His voice dropped a notch as he leaned in. "Calling in one of your favors already?"

Vivi's throat closed. She hadn't meant it like *that*. Heat rushed over her body at the thought of Connor... Of Connor's lips... His hands...

She took a big step back and tried to blot out the image, to shake off the feeling... "You wish." *Ugh.* She'd meant that to sound snappy and flip, but it came out weak and shaky.

Connor's response was another low chuckle that did nothing to help the situation. Then he was heading back to his side of the street without a backward glance, and his casual whistling floated back to her ears. The heat on her skin found a new source. *Damn him.*

This is ridiculous. She was just oversensitive after yesterday, and Connor's attempt to fluster her in the wake of that was adolescent. As was her response, she admitted.

Her butt still hurt, but she couldn't rub the ache away without thinking of Connor's offer. She went to the cooler and grabbed a water bottle and drank deeply, trying to look casual. Her brain began to function normally once she had some distance from him, and she froze in horror as the conversation replayed in her head. Dear Lord, had she really implied that...? And he'd said... And then... *Oh, my God.*

How could her face feel hot while cold chills of horror crawled over her skin? Maybe she was sick. That would truly be excellent: she could claim the earlier conversation was simply feverish ramblings *and* she could spend the rest of Saints and Sinners locked up in her house.

I should be so lucky.

This was what came of trying to be nice to Connor. At least when he was insulting or irritating her he didn't throw little *double entendres* into the conversation to trip her up and mess with her mind.

That explains it. Relief washed over her. She wasn't insane; she just wasn't used to Connor acting like that. He'd taken advantage of her politeness and gotten flirty as if she was just another simpering fan. *That* was what had thrown her off her game. Her world didn't seem quite so off-kilter now. She straightened her shoulders and got ahold of herself. No more Miss Nice-Vivi. It was dangerous.

And how dare he talk to her like she was one of his slobbering, sex-starved groupies? Anger flashed through her. There was a time and a place for that kind of banter and here and now were neither. And she certainly wasn't the right audience. Anger at Connor gave way to anger at herself when a little voice piped up to remind her how quickly she'd jumped to a full-color visual of Connor...

Ugh. Do you have no self-respect at all?

Okay, note to self: no more tossing Connor a rope.

It might end up tied around her neck next time.

Connor had hoped that the physical labor would occupy his mind—or at least focus his thoughts someplace other than south of Vivi's belt. It wasn't working.

What had possessed him to flirt like that with Vivi? After yesterday's awkwardness he shouldn't have said anything even remotely risqué, but neither the words nor Vivi's reaction should have affected him so strongly. A few stupid little remarks, and now all he could think about was Vivi: those long legs, the shapely curve of her butt covered by faded denim clinging to it like a second skin, the way her hands-on-hips stance had called attention to her breasts and the gentle flare of her hips. He'd had a handful of those curves just yesterday, and he was insanely curious to know what they felt like without the fabric separating them from his hands.

Which was totally wrong and crazy because this was

Vivi, for God's sake. Who didn't even like him. More important, he didn't like her.

But, honestly, that was getting harder to justify as well. Vivi hadn't just helped him shoo off the press—who'd spent more time this morning asking about his next album instead of about the news they were actually supposed to be covering—she'd done so in a way guaranteed to make the biggest splash. The image of Vivi in the middle of the street calling him a pretty boy had done more than save him. She'd provided the press with a money shot and the lead to the story.

That could backfire on her and make her look foolish, but it had solved a problem *and* ensured they'd make the local news tonight. They'd probably make several blogs as well.

Vivi was too media-savvy not to know that, so it had to have been her intent. If nothing else, he had to give her props for caring about the cause.

His muscles protested as he hauled an old tire to the refuse pile. This was backbreakingly hard work, especially for someone who'd spent six of the last eight months on the road. Sweat rolled down his spine, and he was glad he'd agreed to do this in January rather than August.

The pain in his wrists and hands reminded him that he probably shouldn't have agreed to this activity at all. He went to the cooler full of water bottles, leaving his hands submerged in the icy water for a few seconds longer than necessary in order to get a little relief.

If he couldn't get his thoughts under control he'd need to be sitting in that ice water soon. And he'd have no one to blame but himself. One thing he was very sure of: Vivi hadn't intended for her words to come across with a double meaning. He'd looked back briefly once safely on his side of the street, just in time to watch all the color drain from her face before she turned bright red. At least the conversation had shaken her, too—if for different reasons.

And *that* knowledge only made his situation worse.

Vivi ignored him for the next few hours, and he returned the favor, refusing to pay any attention to what was going on in her camp until a couple of the Bon Argent board members showed up and waved them both over to inform them of some schedule changes. Vivi was polite and perky until the board members left and they were alone. Then her smile disappeared and she turned abruptly away.

"Vivi—"

She spun and cut him off. "I think it's best if we don't talk. Ever."

"What?"

"Since you can't carry on a civilized and mature conversation on appropriate topics, I'd prefer you not speak to me at all," she said primly.

Vivi was back up on her high horse. "Oh, really?"

"Really."

"Are you this condescending to everyone or just to me?"

Her jaw tightened. "I don't know why we're even attempting a conversation."

He was beginning to agree with her, but before he could say anything Vivi continued.

"You know, I'm not one of your fans, or some reporter you can charm or seduce. I'm not interested, so it doesn't work on me."

That was a slap to his ego. It was also a bald-faced lie, because she wouldn't be so damned upset about it otherwise. "If I had been trying to seduce you, you'd know. The flying pigs would have been a dead give-away."

Vivi's lips all but disappeared as she bit back whatever she wanted to say. Finally, she pried them open again. "Is there an actual reason you stopped me? Or are you just being your usual annoying self?"

"Silly me—I was just trying to be friendly."

"Wow. Your definition of friendly is...insane."

"And *you* need to look up the definitions of *civilized, mature* and *appropriate*. What's gotten your panties all in a twist, anyway?"

Damn it. I shouldn't have brought up her panties.

The look on her face said she agreed—albeit for a different reason. "The condition of my panties is none of your concern."

That was the truth. That reminder didn't help shut down his imagination any, though. "You know, it wouldn't kill you to loosen up some. Relax a little."

"You're giving *me* advice? *You're* supposed to be my role model for lifestyle choices?" With a laugh and a snort that could only be described as disdainful, she added, "Maybe you need to look up *irony* while you've got your dictionary out."

"I think I'm doing pretty well, thank you very damn much."

That eyebrow arched up and it infuriated him.

"I can see where *you'd* think that. *My* goals, however, are a bit higher than just sex, drugs and rock and roll."

"Excuse me?"

She thought for a moment. "No. There's no excuse for you."

For the first time in his life Connor was speechless. Vivi took advantage of the moment, turning on her heel and walking away before he had a chance to gather his wits and rebut.

Vivi could be cold and cutting, and he had no idea what had flipped the switch. He'd actually thought they were making good progress today toward some mutual tolerance.

Boy, were you wrong.

This situation had just crossed into farce territory. He couldn't stop thinking about the panties of a woman who'd just as soon shoot him as look at him. And, since he appreciated and returned the sentiment, the fact he couldn't stop thinking about Vivi and her panties—and the possible lack thereof—was just insult to injury.

This wasn't a farce. It was a nightmare. The very definition of insanity.

How many days left until Mardi Gras?

FIVE

—

Three days later, Vivi was pretty sure she was up to facing Connor again. Well, she was ready to fake it, at least.

Tonight was the Saints and Sinners jazz cruise, and the jazz cruise was corporate money night. Representatives from all the major donors would be there, supposedly to be wooed into opening up their checkbooks. In reality this was just a perk for the donors—another chance to see and be seen and get their pictures in the paper for being good corporate citizens. And she was expected to stand politely next to Connor.

I can do that. Even if it kills me.

Deep down, she was afraid it just might.

No matter how often she reminded herself how much she disliked Connor, *and* repeated her top-ten list of reasons why, she simply could not extinguish that low-grade fire in her belly that had burned all week long. It was bad enough that she couldn't seem to stop thinking about sex, but she could at least rationalize that away because, sadly, her sex life was a bit pitiful at the moment. The disturbing thing was that she couldn't stop thinking about sex with Connor, which was utterly and absolutely insane. She'd spent her entire life *not* thinking about sex with Connor because...well, it was *Connor.*

Maybe once she had small talk and donors to occupy her thoughts, Connor would be forgotten—at least temporarily. She'd be able to make it through the evening then.

A girl can hope.

Dress, wings, shoes, glitter. She'd have to wait until she got to the boat to get dressed. There was no way she could ride in a car in those wings. There were some serious design flaws in that outfit. She'd have to grab one of the servers or someone to help, but she'd worry about that later. She grabbed a lightweight shawl because it would be chilly on the river and carried everything to the living room.

Lorelei sat on the couch, flipping through the paper. She looked up when Vivi entered. "You ready?"

There was no way Lorelei knew just how loaded that question was. "I guess."

"There's a great write-up in here about the work we did Tuesday."

"I know."

"And there's a very *interesting* picture of you and Connor."

She knew that too. What she didn't know was who had taken it. She was horrified to realize that not only had people witnessed their argument, they'd taken a picture—*and* the paper had printed it. So far no one had come forward saying they'd overheard anything, though, and she took small comfort in that much.

"What were you two fighting about anyway?"

Vivi tried to sound casual. "The shape of the earth? The color of the sky? I can't even remember," she lied.

"You're a really bad liar. You know that, right?"

To avoid eye contact, she dug for her lipstick. "He said something about me being uptight, that I needed to relax or something."

"Well, he's not wrong about that."

"Gee, thanks."

"You're running yourself into the ground."

"Between the gallery and Saints and Sinners—"

"And the dozen other organizations that lean on you to get things done, you're busy. I know. It doesn't change the fact that you're letting this town suck you dry. I know you want to be useful. I know you really want to help. But you've surpassed every goal you set out to accomplish. Everyone loves and respects you. They're in awe of you. So give yourself a break."

"I don't have time to take a break."

"Let me ask you something. Do you enjoy all the stuff that you do?"

"It's satisfying and important stuff."

"Yes, but do you *enjoy* it?"

Vivi thought for a second. The answer surprised her. "You know, not as much as I thought I would."

"That's what I suspected. Now, when was the last time you did something for yourself, just because you wanted to? Or went to a party or dinner that didn't have another purpose?"

Vivi couldn't come up with something fast enough to satisfy Lorelei.

Lorelei sighed dramatically. "See? It's Mardi Gras and this whole town is heaving with people here to party and have a good time. But not you."

"Drunken debauchery isn't my idea of a good time."

"And you know this *how*? When was the last time you were drunk or debauched?"

Never. Not even in college. There had always been the worry that it might come back to haunt her. That sounded pitiful, even to her. "I gotta go. I think I hear the car out front."

"Just think about it. You don't have to be a real saint. There's no Miss Perfect title to be won. You don't have to go full-out Sinner, either, but consider being just a little bit bad. It won't kill you. You might even enjoy it."

Like she needed something else on her plate to think about. "And when, exactly, will I fit that into my schedule?"

Lorelei put a hand to her heart and her face melted into disappointed worry. "Oh, Vivi, you're worse than I thought. This has nothing to do with a schedule. You only have one life." Then she smiled and squeezed Vivi's arm. "*Carpe diem,* girl. *Laissez les bon temps rouler.* Enjoy yourself and quit worrying so much about appearances and what other people think."

She was about to go out in public again in a set of freakin' wings. Appearances, indeed. "I'll think about it, okay?"

"I guess that's a start." Lorelei patted her arm. "Have fun tonight. Raise lots of money."

Vivi did think about it on the ride to the dock. Lorelei had a point; even she herself realized that she'd succeeded in her quest and there wasn't anything else to prove. Or anyone to really prove it to.

And for once she was very tempted. She, however, was an expert at resisting temptation. Giving in seemed weak. Anyway, if she did give in who would she be? That was the scary part.

Maybe she could take baby steps in that direction. See how it went before she committed fully.

As the car came to a stop and the driver came around to open her door Vivi shook off Lorelei's words. She had to be the current Vivi tonight and get through Saints and Sinners first.

An hour later the *Mississippi Belle* was packed to the seams as it set off, and Vivi spent far too much energy trying not to bump people with her wings. It was one thing to wear that getup at the ball, but with everyone else here in normal cocktail attire, she felt a little overdressed and awkward.

There were toasts and light snacks before the bands got into the action and people started dancing. Other than the first toast, where she had to stand next to Connor, the mingling kept them far enough apart that her embarrassment over the other day could be kept to a minimum. Connor was enough of a topic of conversation, though, to make her occasionally uncomfortable, but the heat in the room could be blamed for any tell-tale color in her cheeks.

Suddenly a buzz rippled through the crowd, and Vivi turned from her conversation with the mayor to face the stage with everyone else. "What's going on?" she whispered to the lady in front of her.

"Connor Mansfield is going to sing," the woman gushed.

She was sixty if she was a day, and Vivi felt her eyebrows go up when the woman giggled like a teenager. *Every woman alive, indeed.*

Connor mounted the stage to a roar of applause. He'd removed his wings, and the black leather outfit looked far less ridiculous under the spotlights. He looked every inch the rock god, and when he sat at the piano bench Vivi got a good look at his shoulders—all oiled skin stretching over muscle as he flexed his arms and loosened up. *Mercy.* It was a mouthwatering sight.

The collective feminine sigh told her she wasn't alone in her reaction.

"I hadn't really planned on doing this tonight. Just don't tell my agent, okay? She'll expect a cut of the money," Connor joked as he ran his fingers across the keys like he was warming up. "Y'all might know this one," he said with a little smile as he started to play.

The room erupted in applause. Of course the crowd knew the song; "Whiskey and Honey" was one of his biggest hits, and it played almost constantly on the radio.

Connor leaned into the microphone and that sexy baritone filled the room.

He sat down at the bar,
And said, "Gimme what you got,
That'll numb this pain and lie to me tonight."

Vivi willed herself to smile politely and clap along, but her insides were melting. She needed something numbing herself. Connor's voice was whiskey on that low-grade fire, and the heat was building. It just wasn't fair. She'd picked the wrong night to start thinking about being a different Vivi. Damn Lorelei for putting ideas about being bad in her head. That idea kept swirling around with the other bad thoughts in her head and that was very dangerous.

She said, "Honey, what you need,
Is something we've got.
Sit right on back—"

Vivi tried to make her way to the other side of the room as unobtrusively as possible, but her stupid wings kept bumping people. Thankfully almost everyone was enthralled with Connor's performance and the interruption was shrugged off.

Then Connor launched into the chorus.

She served a little whiskey and honey.
It goes down real easy when you drink it slow.
She can stop a heart and free a weary soul.
She sang a lot like whiskey...whiskey and honey.

The whole room was singing now, and Vivi felt a stab of something between anger and jealousy. It was a nice change from the earlier confusion. This was Connor's event now. He owned it as surely as he owned

the crowd. She wanted to be angry at him for grabbing the spotlight and making tonight about him, but
at the same time she was jealous he was able to do it
so easily. And everyone in the room was glad he did.
They felt special now: the lucky few attendees at a
private concert.

Think of the positives. Connor was giving the crowd
what they wanted, and in return the crowd would
donate money—even more than they'd originally
planned.

She actually wasn't upset at Connor's showboating,
or jealous of his popularity. He was right to be working the angles he had.

No, it just made her situation worse. Her personal
situation. She was lusting after a man she couldn't
have. Dear heaven, Connor was the one man she
shouldn't be lusting after at all. The sound of his voice
washed over her, fanning those flames and making it
hard to focus on anything else.

She was pitiful. Pathetic. Insane.

She pushed open the door to the deck; getting outside would lessen the shock and sensations. The cool
air helped some, but not enough.

One week down. Three to go.

She wasn't going to make it.

Three songs and his hands were burning. He was
supposed to be resting them, letting the inflamma-
tion subside and heal. So much for that idea. At least
he'd been able to leave it at three, turning the stage
and spotlight back over to the band.

Connor held his beer in one hand, letting the cold

soothe that hand some before switching and giving the other a little relief. It wasn't ideal, but it helped and did so in an unobtrusive way. The banker talking to him had no idea—which was fair, he thought, because Connor really hadn't been listening and had no idea what he was talking about.

He was dripping sweat from his performance, and the heat from the mass of bodies in the room kept him from cooling down. "Can you excuse me? I'm going to step outside and cool off."

"Sure thing. Maybe we could talk later about my idea?"

Damn. He should have listened a bit more carefully. God only knew what the banker—whose name he didn't even know—might have in mind. Thankfully he was saved from having to make even the most noncommittal of commitments by the arrival of a slightly drunk woman who stumbled over the banker and spilled her drink onto his shirt. Connor used the distraction to slip out the side door.

The air cooled him immediately and the breeze off the river helped dry the sweat. It felt good.

He wasn't the only one escaping the crowd. Small groups of people lined the railings, but it was much quieter out here. The music inside was muted by the walls, the thrumming of the engines and the splashes of the big paddle wheel. The breeze carried conversations out over the river, making the deck feel more private and isolated than it really was. Meanwhile, the lights of the city looked as lively as ever, even from this distance, and he inhaled the sights and smells of home.

He made his way toward the back of the boat, away

from the windows, lest anyone inside see him outside alone and think he needed company. He threw a glance over his shoulder as he turned the corner and bumped into something. He turned quickly, and feathers hit him in the mouth.

Vivi jumped, apologizing before she'd fully turned around. When she saw it was him, the words died in an instant. She stepped away and awkwardness settled around her as he felt the tension rise. That wasn't anger, either. It was tension relating to the *other* things that had happened this week. Seemed she wasn't quite past that yet.

Oddly, neither was he. It didn't seem as cold out here now.

"Show over already?"

"Should I be insulted that you didn't stick around to listen?"

Vivi snorted. "I'm sure no one noticed *my* absence."

Like he'd been asking for the additional attention. "Why are you hiding back here?"

"It's noisy and hot inside. I needed a break, so I slipped out for a minute."

Vivi had a shawl wrapped around her, but it couldn't be doing much good, hiked up over her wings like it was. It covered her arms, but he could see her shivering. She'd been out here longer than a minute or two.

"You should go back inside. You're turning blue."

"I'm perfectly fine." Her chin lifted regally, but her chattering teeth ruined the effect.

"Seriously, you look like Angel Smurf."

Vivi set her shoulders. "Is there a reason you're out here looking for me? If not, just butt out. I'm a big girl and I'll go back inside when I'm good and ready." She'd raised her voice to a near shout, and a door opened behind them and a crew member carrying a box exited to give them a strange look before scurrying away. Vivi cleared her throat and smiled. "Thank you for your concern, but I'm good."

In other words Vivi would stand here until she began suffering from exposure just to spite him. And for some reason that pure, completely irrational stubbornness infuriated him. Connor caught the door with his foot before it closed and reached for Vivi's arm.

"What the—?" Vivi sputtered as he pulled her inside.

The door slammed with a satisfying bang. The little storage room was quiet except for the throb of the engines and nominally warmer. Her grinned at her. "At least stand out of the wind."

"You are insufferable, Connor Mansfield." She tried to move past him, but he blocked her. Her eyes narrowed dangerously. "Move, or I will kill you where you stand."

"Sorry. I can't let you be an idiot."

"What difference does it make to you?"

He paused. *Excellent question*. "If you end up in the hospital with pneumonia, you'll have to forfeit the competition."

"That's ridiculous."

"Warm up in here or go back inside. It's up to you."

"Why the hell do you care so much?"

"Because you're acting like a two-year-old instead of a grown woman."

Her jaw tightened. "But I *am* a grown woman, and

therefore able to decide when I'm cold. New Orleans isn't exactly the Arctic Circle. I think I can survive a few minutes outside without frostbite."

Good Lord, were they really fighting about the temperature? He chuckled, and Vivi shot him a look.

"What's so funny?"

"You'd argue the earth was flat just because I said it was round."

Vivi's lips pressed together as the truth and ridiculousness of the situation was clarified for her. She cleared her throat and lifted her chin again. "Possibly. I do like a lively debate."

"You just like to try to prove me wrong."

She shrugged, but there was a smile tugging at her lips. "That too."

This current scene, playing out in all of its ridiculousness, proved that they really couldn't go on like this. It would make them both crazy, and it held zero appeal. "How about a cease-fire?" he said.

That got her attention in a big way, and he had no idea why.

"Excuse me?"

"Just until this Saints and Sinners thing is over. We're going to have to be around each other and the constant battling is giving me a headache."

Shock caused her jaw to drop, so he softened it with a promise.

"You can go back to hating me with a passion on Ash Wednesday."

"That rather defeats the purpose. You know that half the interest this year comes from the fact we're well-known to be adversarial."

That was true. Vivi's little showdown at the cleanup site on Tuesday had been the lead in every news item about Saints and Sinners. "I didn't say we had to become best friends. Just a small attempt at tolerance so I don't have to watch my back all the time."

Vivi seemed to find the proposition amusing for some reason, but she finally nodded. "I agree. Now, in the spirit of this cease-fire, will you please step aside?"

He bowed deep from the waist and stepped aside. "Of course."

Vivi nearly hit him with her wings again as she put her hands against the door and pushed. The door didn't open. She pushed again, harder, but nothing happened.

She turned to him. "A little help, please?"

He tried, but the door wouldn't open. A second, harder push also accomplished nothing. He cursed, and Vivi looked at him sharply.

"It can't be locked."

"It's either locked or stuck. Either way, it's not opening."

"What kind of door locks people inside?"

He was thinking the same thing. The door was smooth and blank on this side, and he couldn't locate any kind of mechanism to explain why the door wouldn't open now. "It must lock from the outside somehow."

"It wasn't locked a minute ago."

"True."

Vivi turned sharply, smacking him with her wings again. "Oh, damn it. That guy was carrying a box when he came out. I bet he came back and threw the lock."

"That's as good an explanation as any."

"This is going to be embarrassing." She thought for a minute, then sighed. "Who can you call that will come unlock the door? *Discreetly*," she added.

"No one." At her look, he added, "I'm not exactly close friends with anyone on this boat."

That got him another sigh. "Let me think. Caroline McGee is here, and I'm pretty sure I know her number. I'll never live this down, but she'll be less likely to make a big production out of it. Can I borrow your phone?"

"Where's yours?"

"In my purse in the dining room. Why are you being difficult?"

"Because mine is in my jacket in the dining room as well."

Her eyebrows went up. "You're kidding me."

He pointed to his very tight leather pants. "No pockets."

Vivi cursed a blue streak that would have been amusing in a different situation. "Okay, this is going to be so embarrassing, but..." She made a fist and beat against the door. "*Hey! Help!* There are people trapped in here!"

He leaned against the steel wall and let her bang until she stopped and rubbed her hand. "Do you really think anyone will hear you?"

"Yes, I do."

"Everyone is at the other end of the boat. There's a band, the engine noise..."

"Then break it down." She waved a hand toward the door. "I'll pay for the damage."

"Break it down? Are you crazy?"

"Be all macho. Put your shoulder into it."

"It's a metal door, Vivi. No one's that macho."

"So we're just stuck in here?"

"People are bound to miss us eventually. We're not exactly just part of the crowd tonight. They'll come looking."

"Great. I'm going to die in a storage room." She rubbed a hand over her eyes.

"Relax. We're not going to die in here. Worst case scenario is that we have to wait until we dock and the engines are turned off. Someone will hear us shouting then."

Vivi started pacing. The wings were smacking against everything—including him—but at least she would be warming up some with the exercise.

"This is your fault, you know," she snapped.

It was his turn to sigh at her. "So much for that truce."

"That was agreed *before* you got me trapped in a freakin' closet."

"*I* didn't lock the door."

"No, but you pulled me in here. Therefore it's your fault."

He threw his hands up. "Fine. It's my fault. I'm very sorry, Vivi, and you can berate me all you like."

Vivi merely frowned at him in response.

He looked around with the vague notion there might be something in here of help, but it was just a storage closet. Boxes of dishes and glasses were stacked neatly on shelves next to bundles of cloth napkins. With no other options, he sat on the floor and leaned against the metal wall to wait.

"What are you doing?"

"Getting comfortable. You might as well have a seat."

"I'll pass, thank you." She crossed her arms and adjusted the shawl.

"The floor's not that dirty. You can even grab one of those napkins if you're worried about your dress."

Vivi shot him a withering look, and he realized the problem: her wings. The wings were hard to sit in, but it could be done. In a chair, at least. On the floor it would be impossible. "Want me to help you get your wings off?"

"No. I'll just stand."

Vivi couldn't even lean properly against something with those wings in the way. Unless, of course, she wanted to lean face-forward against the wall. Connor laughed to himself at the visual. He looked at Vivi's dress carefully, visualizing the wings' harness. Assuming hers was designed similarly to his, she'd have to strip to the waist to get them off. Her refusal made a little sense then, but he couldn't believe her modesty would go that far.

"Let me know if you change your mind."

"I will."

He kind of hoped she would. Or that she wouldn't. Being locked in a closet with Vivi—much less a half-naked Vivi—was dangerous and confusing territory. Maybe it would be best if she didn't. He would just hope they weren't stuck in here for very long.

Vivi paced and Connor stared at the walls. Time

slowed to a crawl, and without a watch or his phone he had no idea how long they'd been in there. The silence and tension were palpable things, but he was bored out of his mind. "Talk about *déjà vu*."

Vivi jumped at the break in the silence. "Excuse me?"

"Mike Delacroix's party—sophomore year. We played Seven Minutes in Heaven, remember? Although in our case, it was more like Three Minutes of Insults Followed by Four Minutes of Stony Silence." He chuckled, but Vivi's look clearly said she didn't share his amusement at the memory.

"How could I forget that? It was one of the most humiliating moments of my life."

"You've led a charmed life, then."

"Oh, shut up. I could have easily forgotten those seven minutes and lived them down if you hadn't told Julie Hebert how I threw myself at you and how awful it was."

"I did no such thing." He might have been a juvenile ass, but that was just simply untrue and he felt unfairly vilified.

"No one would believe *my* story that nothing happened, and Andy Ackerman broke up with me the next day for cheating on him."

"So *that's* what happened between you two." At her frown, he added, "You know that Julie wanted Andy for herself."

"Duh. They started going out a week later."

"Not that it makes a difference now, but I never said anything to Julie Hebert about anything. The girl was a viper."

"She still is."

"But you don't believe me?"

She shrugged, but it was tight, not casual. "As you said, it doesn't make a difference now."

"Then why bring it up?"

"*You're* the one who brought it up."

"*I* was just trying to make conversation."

She rolled her eyes again. "How 'bout them Saints?"

He took the hint. "They had a decent season. I missed most of it, of course. The NFL doesn't get a lot of airtime in Europe."

"Pity." Vivi was shifting from one foot to the other. Her legs had to be getting tired. She reached around, experimenting with the wings' position, but they didn't move much. Certainly not enough for her to get comfortable at all.

He let it continue for a few minutes before trying again. "Seriously, Vivi. Let me help you get those off."

She hesitated, and he expected another refusal.

"Fine." Her voice was pained.

It took him a second to move past the surprise that she'd agreed to his help. He levered himself up off the floor as Vivi turned her back to him. A row of hooks ran from the neckline, down her back, and ended a few inches below her waist. Vivi couldn't have gotten out of this alone if she'd wanted to. He wondered who'd gotten her into it in the first place.

He undid the three hooks above the place where her wings connected, carefully keeping his fingers away from her skin, and the shoulder straps of her dress loosened and sagged.

Vivi's hands came up to grab the bodice and hold it against her chest.

The hooks underneath the wings were harder to undo, but soon he was staring at the bare length of Vivi's spine from the wings all the way down to the lacy trim on her panties. She had a lovely back, the musculature defined without looking sharp or harsh. His fingers were an inch away from tracing that line of her spine before he caught himself. *Not a good idea. Behave like a gentleman.*

Vivi's breathing had turned shallow, causing her ribs to move only the tiniest bit with each breath. His own ribs felt too tight against his lungs, and it got even harder to breathe as Vivi pulled her arms out of the dress.

He couldn't help her get her shoulders out of the harness without touching her, and the cool softness of her skin seemed to sear his fingers. One hand clutched the fabric over her breasts as she pulled her arm through the first strap. She seemed to be holding her breath as they quickly repeated the action on the other side.

Then he released the hooks of the strap around her ribs and the wings fell into his hands. He set the wings aside as Vivi shrugged the dress straps back over her shoulders.

Red lines marred her skin, and without thinking he ran his hands over them to soothe the pain. Vivi gasped at the touch, bringing him quickly back to his senses.

His hands were shaking like a teenager's as he quickly re-hooked the dress. Goosebumps covered her skin—from the cold or something else? he wondered. When he stepped back Vivi didn't turn around immediately, instead taking her time wrapping her shawl around her. With a casualness he didn't really feel, he returned to his former seat and tried to get comfortable again.

That was impossible, and he ended up bending his leg at the knee to camouflage the evidence that the ridiculous leather pants seemed to want to advertise.

"Thank you." Vivi's voice was as thin as air. "That feels much better."

He swallowed hard. "You're welcome."

Vivi pulled a couple of napkins off the shelf and laid them carefully on the floor. Then she sat, her back against the locked door. It wasn't an ideal position, but the only other option would be to sit next to him. At this moment he was happy she'd chosen to face him instead. She wrapped her shawl tight around her shoulders before leaning back. She wouldn't meet his eyes, focusing instead on the fringed edge of her shawl, straightening the strings into neat, precise lines.

The tension and silence were now suffocating.

How much longer until they were found?

SIX

—

Every breath Vivi took felt like glass cutting into her lungs. She felt drained from bouncing from emotion to emotion, but oddly electrified at the same time. It was disturbing.

Connor said he wanted her to warm up. Well, she'd accomplished that in spades. Between embarrassment and lust, she might burn to ashes long before anyone ever rescued them.

She was glad to have the wings off, glad to be able to finally sit down, but once again she was trapped in a small, enclosed space with Connor. And between the last few days of inappropriate thoughts and the touch of his hands against her skin she was primed and nearly shaking with need.

She clasped her hands together until the knuckles turned white, but she kept them in her lap where they belonged.

Connor's hands, she noted, were on his thighs, splaying out in a stretch before he curled them back into loose fists. As she watched, he did it again. She let her eyes cut to his face and saw his jaw tighten.

"Something wrong with your hands?" The words were out before she realized it.

His eyes flew to hers. "What?"

There was something in his voice, but it was a simple question so she didn't back down. "You're moving them like they're cramped or something, and you look like you're in pain."

He was quiet for a moment, examining them, then he shrugged. "It's tendonitis. I'm supposed to be resting them, not banging away like Jerry Lee Lewis."

"Then why did you play?"

An eyebrow cocked up. "Because how could I say no?"

"Easy. You say, 'No, I'm supposed to be resting my hands'."

"Gee, why didn't I think of that?"

The sarcasm caught her off guard, and it took a second for her to put the pieces together. "I see. You don't want anyone to know."

"Bingo." He clasped his hands together and let them rest in his lap. "So I'd appreciate it if you kept this information to yourself."

He seemed so serious she answered, "I will," immediately. She met his eyes to show she meant it. "But can I ask why?"

"Because."

Men. "It's an injury, not a personal failing."

"This is my career, Vivi. I don't need something—however minor it may seem—overshadowing me."

"Can't stand the shadows, can you? Gotta be the superstar."

Connor shot her an irritated look, but shrugged instead of biting back.

She regretted the words instantly. Music was Connor's life—it always had been—and now, just when he was reaping success for his work, he was facing a problem that could jeopardize that success. Being told he couldn't play music would be like asking him not to breathe. If the situation were reversed, she'd be freaking out over the possibility. She was ashamed of herself for making light of it, even for a second.

"I'm sorry. That snark was uncalled for."

"Old habits die hard."

"True. But look at it this way," she offered in her best perky voice, "*I'm* the one person you can trust not to blow sunshine up your skirt. If there was a way for me to give you grief about this, you know I'd do it in a heartbeat. But I'm coming up empty. If it's impossible for *me,* then people who actually *like* you won't be able to make anything of it either."

Connor shook his head in amused disbelief. "The fact you're right about that seems unbelievably wrong."

"See, you thought having a mortal enemy was a *bad* thing." She crossed her feet at the ankles and looked at him with all the innocence she could muster. "Any other hard truths you need hearing? I've got nothing better to do, thanks to you."

Connor's eyebrows went up. "Sounds like I owe you a hard truth or two."

Ugh. Return of high school trauma. "I'll pass, thanks."

"Scared, Vivi?"

"Hardly." She tried to wave it off like it was nothing. "I don't need you to give me a hard time. I have Lorelei for that."

Connor had the nerve to cluck at her.

I will not take the bait. It might kill her, but she wasn't opening herself up to Connor's derision. She wasn't stupid. "Any idea how long we've been in here?"

"None."

How frustrating. "You know, you'd think someone would have noticed you were missing by now."

"Just me? You're not exactly incognito tonight, Saint Vivienne."

"But you're the star attraction."

"Jealous?"

"Not at all." Oddly, she meant it. "You've earned your adulation and all the perks that come with that. We mere mortals just do the best we can."

Connor's laugh was sharp and mocking. "'Mere mortals?' Please. Let me tell you something, since we're sharing hard truths tonight. If I have to hear one more person sing *your* praises, I just might puke."

"My praises? Yeah, right."

"'Vivi is so *giving* and *selfless* and *hardworking,*'" he gushed in a singsong voice. "'She does so *much* for the community. Don't know *what* we'd do without her...' Blah, blah, blah. I'm surprised they haven't built a freakin' statue in your honor in Jackson Square."

"Seriously?"

"Seriously. We mere mortals who lack your saintly perfection are rather sick of it."

A happy glow started in her chest. "Wow. Thanks."

"That wasn't a compliment," he grumped.

"But I'm taking it as such, and I won't let you take it back, either."

"Only you."

"Only me, what?"

Connor merely shrugged.

His attitude damped her happy glow and nearly snapped her temper. "You know, just because you don't like me, you shouldn't be so shocked that others do."

He crossed his arms over his chest. "You certainly seem shocked that folks might like *me* even though you don't."

"No, I know exactly why people like you. You're charming and glib and talented. You're also quite handsome."

"Why, thank you, Vivi."

He said it so grudgingly she wanted to smack him. "Like I said, there are plenty of reasons for people to like you. I'm just not that shallow. And I know you better than that."

"Oh, really?"

"Uh-huh. You're charming because it gets you what you want from people, and you're glib because you don't really care all that much. You're crazy talented— I won't deny that. And I know you've worked hard, so I give you proper credit there, too. I also know you can be very petty, extremely superficial and completely self-centered. Oh, and your ego is suffocatingly immense." *Wow, saying that felt good.*

"While, you, Miss Vivi, are sanctimonious and supercilious. You are dismissive to anyone or anything that doesn't meet *your* standards. And I don't know what's more insufferable—your pride or your supe-riority complex."

They were trading insults, but it still hurt. "You're the insufferable one. Plus, you're...mean."

"Mean?" He snorted. "Great, now we're ten years old again."

"No, when we were ten we were still sort of friends. It wasn't until puberty that you became a jerk."

"All teenage boys are jerks. It's called testosterone."

She nearly choked on her temper. "*That's* your ex-cuse? Testosterone?"

"It's an explanation, not an excuse."

"You're such a jerk, you can't even apologize."

"Hi, Pot. I'm Kettle. I think we're on equal ground, sweetheart."

The condescending "sweetheart" broke her hold on the last strings of her temper. "Two words—Marie Lester."

"Who?"

"Wow, you don't even remember. That's pitiful." She didn't care if she sounded sanctimonious. She had rea-son to be. "Marie Lester—the girl from Alabama who moved here junior year."

"Oh, yeah. What about her?"

"You used me to get to her for no reason other than to stroke your ego. You made me your accomplice. And you played—" She stopped before she let the rest of that out. "That's a character flaw that can't be chalked up to testosterone."

"*That's* why you slapped me at coronation?"

"Uh-huh. You deserved it."

"And you're still stewing over that? That's some grudge you've got going on there."

"Marie was my friend, and she never forgave me."

"She moved away the next year."

"That's not the point."

"Then what *is* your point, Vivi?"

"I have yet to see any real reason to believe that's not still part of your personality. You came to me looking for a cease-fire then, too. You took me to the movies, walked me home from school..." She choked on the words. "Then I found out I was nothing more than a means to an end. And neither then nor now do you see the problem with that."

He leveled a stare at her until the silence became tense. "You're right. That was a jerk move. I will offer a blanket apology for everything that happened from the time we were twelve until we were twenty-five. Teenagers—specifically teenage boys—are a different breed. I probably was a jerk. But now that my frontal lobe is fully developed I would really like to quit being condemned based on something that happened years ago."

That was an eye-opening concession on Connor's part. Vivi was about to accept and offer an apology of her own when he opened his mouth again.

"What's your excuse, Vivi?"

He just couldn't quit while he was ahead. That was good. It worked wonders at negating all those earlier conflicting feelings and disturbing thoughts.

"I've had just about enough of this fun for tonight." Vivi pushed to her feet and banged on the door, calling for help until her hands throbbed and her throat felt scratchy. No one came. She leaned against it in defeat and let her head fall back. "This is a nightmare."

Connor stacked his hands behind his head and grinned at her. "Some women would consider being locked in with me a dream come true." Mercy, he really did look just like Satan, dangling temptation.

She closed her eyes against the sight. "They're deluded. And stupid."

"This isn't exactly my idea of a fun time either."

Vivi scrubbed her hands over her face. "God, this is going to be even worse than Mike Delacroix's party."

"*This* was an accident."

"So we *say*. We're hiding in a closet in the middle of a party. How we got locked in that closet doesn't matter beyond the humor factor. No one's going to believe that this was totally innocent, and I'm a laughingstock either way."

"You're overreacting."

"Oh, really?" His condescending nod had her fingernails digging into her palms as she kept her fists at her sides. "No one's going to believe that you dragged me in here, so I will be the assumed dragg*er* instead of the drag*ee*. If nothing happened after I dragged you into a closet, it's obvious that you're immune to my advances. Cue the laughter at my expense. If something did happen, then I'm just another one of Connor Mansfield's many groupies. Either way you win, I lose. It's tenth grade all over again. At least I don't have a boyfriend to dump me this time." She banged her head against the door gently.

"You're right, Vivi."

"Pardon me if that admission doesn't exactly fill me with the glee and satisfaction it normally would."

"We'll just tell everyone that I dragged you in here to seduce you, but you declined the offer."

"Like anyone would believe *that*."

"You can punch me in the face. The bruise should be enough proof."

"Don't tempt me."

He stood and lifted his chin, daring her. "Go ahead. Take a shot. You can't tell me you're not dying to anyway. I'll look like a horn dog and your virtue will be redeemed."

There had to be a trap here someplace. "But why would you do that?"

"Because in the grand scheme of things one musician trying to seduce one beautiful girl really isn't news."

"Why would you decide to seduce *me*? And why now after all these years?"

There was that little smirk again. "Maybe the groupies aren't as plentiful as you seem to believe."

"Yeah, right."

"Why is it so hard to believe that I'm not *that* indiscriminate about my sexual partners?"

"Because that's not what I heard."

His jaw tightened. She'd hit a nerve. "Yeah, well a lot of people have heard that. That doesn't make it true. And the woman has been proved a liar."

"Only in that you didn't father her baby."

"I can't say for certain that I never met the woman, because I meet a lot of people, but I think I'd remember sleeping with her. Especially considering her description of the event."

"You're telling me it's inaccurate?"

"I'm not sure half of what she claimed happened is even possible. And if it is possible, it probably shouldn't be legal."

He certainly seemed sincere. "So why take the paternity test?"

"Denials weren't making it—or her—go away. Do you know how damn hard it is to prove you *didn't* do something?"

It would be. People liked to believe the worst. Plus, Connor had no reason to lie to her, of all people. It wasn't as if he really worried about what she thought of him. Strangely, though, it made a difference to her to know he wasn't some kind of player, regardless of the rumors. She didn't like the fact that it *did* make a difference, though.

"Want to know why famous people usually date other famous people?" Connor asked.

"So you can be fabulous together?"

"No. It's self-protection in the form of mutual annihilation. When you have nothing to gain and a lot to lose, you're more likely to keep your mouth shut."

Vivi had nothing to say to that. It was a sad state of affairs, and she felt a stab of pity. It must have shown on her face because Connor scowled at her.

"It still doesn't mean anyone would believe you'd try to seduce me. I'm not famous, and everyone knows you don't even like me," she said.

"But who would blame me for trying? Vivi LaBlanc is the city's sweetheart. Smart, beautiful...saintly.

Sexy. People would question my masculinity if I didn't at least try, right?"

There was a bit of snark behind the words, but not enough to completely counter the funny effect they had on her insides. She tried to ignore them. "You're laying it on pretty thick, don't you think?"

His voice dropped a notch. "You're assuming none of it is true. And I can be very convincing when I need to be. You'll be the envy of half the women in the city, yet retain the respect of all."

A shiver ran over her. "Except for the ones who'll think I was stupid to pass up the chance."

"Well, we all must live with regrets."

Connor's voice was hypnotic, and his eyes were hooded as they roamed over her. It would be too easy forget it was part of the overall act, the cover story to salvage her pride.

"You are beautiful, Vivi. Your hair... Your eyes... Your skin." His fingers followed his words. "Your mouth—including that sharp tongue—is enough to drive a man crazy." Connor's lips quirked up. "In more ways than one, that is."

Those talented fingers traced over her shoulder and down her arm. Tingles danced across her skin and her blood felt thick in her veins. It might not be real, but her body didn't know the difference and her mind was happy to play along ignorantly. The air felt close and heavy, and she couldn't hear the engines above the thudding of her own pulse. She watched the rise and fall of Connor's chest as the weight of his stare and the silence built to a crushing level that made her knees weak.

Connor leaned forward, his chest barely brushing hers each time they breathed, and his head dropped until his lips were level to her ear. The slight breeze of his breath over the lobe sent a shiver arcing all the way to her core as a hand snaked around her waist to her lower back, edging her closer. The hard lines of Connor's body seared into hers. The air turned thick, each breath filling her lungs with his scent.

"You could tempt a saint, Vivi, much less a simple sinner like me. Resistance is a battle. One I'm not sure I want to win." He paused, letting the words hang, and her hand floated up of its own accord to land on his chest. The muscle leapt at her touch and she could feel the thump of his heart against her palm. An ache started to build in her core.

"Ready to punch me now?"

The words were a bucket of cold water that doused the rising heat and left shame in its place. She shoved him away.

Connor stumbled and caught himself on the wall. Righting himself, he shook like a wet dog and focused on her face. "You were supposed to hit me. A shove won't leave a bruise."

"Just shut up." She swallowed hard. She'd never hit another human being before, didn't think she'd be capable of it, but Connor might be the one to change all of that. Not because of what he'd done, but because of her reaction to it.

She took a deep breath, but whether it was to calm herself or prepare herself to berate him she'd never know, because cold air rushed in as the door opened. The same crew member from earlier stood there with his mouth open. The shock seemed to ricochet off the metal walls.

Connor recovered first. "We thought you'd never come back."

"I j-just needed to get some glasses..." He started to step back outside.

Vivi scanned the deck behind him. Empty. Thankfully it was just the three of them. No one else was there to witness this. She cleared her throat and smiled at the gaping man. "Connor and I stepped in here to speak privately out of the wind, not realizing you'd be back to lock the door. We've been shouting, but no one could hear us."

His face reddened. "I'm *so* sorry, Miss LaBlanc, Mr. Mansfield."

"Not as sorry as we are." Connor grinned at the young man. "But no harm, no foul. We won't mention this if you won't."

The threat was subtle, but the young man caught it and nodded. "Of course. I appreciate it. I don't want to get into trouble with the captain."

Connor grabbed Vivi's wings and held the door for her to step through. The man stood there, probably in shock, but possibly a little starstruck too, as they left. The wind had picked up while they were locked away, and it blew Vivi's hair into her face. While that would normally be annoying, Vivi didn't try to right it. It meant she didn't have to look at Connor.

"You go on inside," he said as they walked. "I'll follow in a minute or two. If anyone asks, don't deny you were with me. Just don't say where. If that guy decides to talk later, a denial you were ever with me will make you look guilty." She nodded, and he handed her the wings. "Don't worry. I don't think it's going to be a problem. And if it becomes one, we'll just go back to the other plan."

"You're serious?"

"Vivi, I never say anything I don't mean. Now, go."

The noise of the party seemed ten times louder after being in that closet for so long. But no one gave her a second glance as she left her wings by the door and went to the bar for a glass of water. People spoke to her as she made her way through the crowd, but it was the same basic chatter. No one seemed to have noticed she and Connor had been rather conspicuously absent at the same time. Relief rushed through her as she pushed open the door to the ladies' room and checked her reflection. Other than a slight pinkness to her cheeks and a rather chaotic hairstyle—both of which could be chalked up to the wind on deck—nothing looked amiss.

I never say anything I don't mean. She thought about everything Connor *had* said and the statement began to sound vaguely ominous—if only because of her reaction to his words. Just replaying those moments in her mind had her nipples tightening against the silk lining of her dress and her thighs clenching in anticipation.

This is not good. Not good at all.

She pressed a hand to her belly to calm the butterflies there. She might not have a public problem, but she sure as hell had a private one.

They'd been locked in that closet for over an hour. It had felt like a lifetime, but with several hundred people

on board—and the flow of cocktails probably helped—
no one had found it noteworthy that neither he nor
Vivi had been seen for a while. Everyone had just assumed the two of them were someplace else—not necessarily together, because...well, why *would* they be?
Connor didn't bother to correct any assumptions.

When they finally docked, he and Vivi were forced
back into the shared spotlight in a reverse receiving
line. Though they were side by side, Vivi kept her attention on the guests, barely throwing a single glance
his way.

Then, with a simple "See ya," Vivi followed the last
guest down the gangplank.

Normally Connor wouldn't have given it a second
thought, but Vivi had been in his thoughts a lot recently. And after tonight... Well, Vivi was pretty much
all he could think about, and none of it made any sense
at all.

The chauffeur dropped him in front of Gabe's building. There had been huge crowds of revelers on Bourbon, but the crowds were thinner here, and most of
the people were either too intoxicated or too focused
on their own good time to pay him any notice at all.

Good, because I'm really not in the mood tonight.

The kind of mood he was in was easy to pinpoint
and name. His whole body thrummed with want, but
it was a specific want. *Vivi.* And that didn't make any
sense at all.

Why now? Why after all these years did he suddenly
have the hots for Vivi LaBlanc? He'd crossed a line tonight, taken everything a step too far, and the next

thing he knew he'd had Vivi in his arms, just seconds from kissing her.

While he tried to remind himself that Vivi was his self-proclaimed mortal enemy, she'd certainly shown a new side of herself to him tonight—in between insults, at least. And when he tried to remind himself that he didn't like Vivi—had never liked Vivi—his body was quick to argue that wasn't entirely true. Her confession that had stopped just short of admitting that she might have had different feelings toward him once upon a time didn't help either.

The normal litany of reasons he could usually recite failed him. Insanity was the only explanation that made sense.

He dropped his keys on the table and propped his wings against the wall. At least he wouldn't have to wear this outfit again until Fat Tuesday. Grabbing a beer from the fridge, he drank half of it in one long swallow as he went to the bathroom and pulled off the leather pants and vest. A long, slightly cooler than normal shower helped him clear his head and focus, but it did nothing to take the edge off.

Sleep was out of the question, so he pulled on a pair of sweats and went to the kitchen for another beer. He could see himself needing several tonight. And if the mental replay couldn't be stopped, he'd need another, much colder shower soon.

The intercom buzzed loudly in the silence. It was most likely a lost tourist or random drunk, but he answered anyway.

"It's Vivi."

His hand slammed the release button before the

words were even completely out of her mouth. He didn't bother to question why she'd suddenly appeared, didn't really care. The jolt to his system caused by her voice honed that earlier dull edge to painful sharpness. As he opened the door to the stairwell, he heard the outside door close and the sounds of feet on the stairs. It was the sound of a slow climb, but a purposeful one. When Vivi rounded the last landing she looked up and saw him. Her feet seemed to stall, and she climbed the last flight at a snail's pace, not quite holding eye contact, but not staring at her feet either. She'd changed from the satin column of her Saint costume into jeans and a battered jacket zipped up to her neck.

She blew her hair out of her face. "Thanks for letting me in. I wasn't sure you would."

"It's one o'clock in the morning. I couldn't leave you standing on the street." That was a good enough explanation. And until he knew her reason for coming by in the middle of the night...

Connor realized he was holding his breath.

On the top stair, Vivi stopped, and he noticed her knuckles turning white as her fingers gripped the banister. She was totally still, except for the rapid rise and fall of her chest. Out of breath from the climb? Or...?

She didn't move, so Connor didn't either. He stayed in the doorway, leaning against the door frame. The silence stretched out. Finally he couldn't take it anymore. "Why are you here, Vivi?"

Vivi's eyes flew to his. *Damn.* That came out sharper than he'd intended. Then that flush began to climb out of the collar of her jacket again.

"I—I don't really know." She sighed, and he thought

he heard a small curse. "You know, I probably shouldn't have come. I'm sorry I bothered you."

She turned and started slowly back down the stairs.

Let her go. It's really better to just— Even as he was thinking the thoughts his feet were moving, closing the space between them, and he was at the top of the stairs before she'd taken more than a couple.

"Vivi."

She turned, and he held out his hand. It was her choice. He couldn't make it for her, but she'd come this far and he felt like he needed to meet her halfway. She hesitated, then put her hand in his.

He hauled her up the last few stairs and pulled her body against his. He could feel her tension, but their bodies seemed to fit together like puzzle pieces and the sensation was electric.

Vivi's eyes widened at the contact, and he knew she felt the same electricity. She swallowed hard, then he felt the slow slide of her chest against his as she rose up on her toes and aligned her mouth evenly with his.

There was the smallest moment of hesitation—one breath's worth—and then her lips touched his.

He never knew what to expect from Vivi, and this was no different. Her mouth was pliant and warm, but cautious, gently moving against his.

Every rational thought shouted at him to stop. This was Vivi, and he had no business kissing her. He shouldn't want to.

But he couldn't have stopped if he tried. She tasted fresh, sweet and, God help him, *right*. Her tongue slid past his lips, and the tentative touch awakened something primal inside him, beating down all the rational thoughts until he couldn't imagine not kissing her.

Vivi's fingers threaded through his hair as his hands splayed over her back, pulling her weight onto his chest, and he felt the change in her as the kiss turned carnal and needy.

Without breaking contact, he backed up the few feet into the apartment and let the door swing closed. The sound punctuated the moment as a point of no return. He couldn't say what exactly had changed between them, or when or why, but the wall had been crumbling and the kiss had reduced it to rubble. It defied reason, but it somehow made perfect sense.

"Vivi—"

She stopped him by pressing a finger against his lips, and he lost his train of thought when those blue eyes met his. The clear evidence of desire he saw there just threw gasoline on to the bonfire.

She swallowed hard and her voice was barely above a whisper. "Could we not...actually...talk? I'm about to lose my nerve, and I really don't want to."

He should follow up, not just let that statement slide, but Vivi was kissing him again, and nothing else seemed to matter.

Vivi didn't want to think, didn't want to examine this too closely, because if she did, she'd realize what a fool she was. She just hadn't been able to shake his words or the feelings those words evoked. Coupled with the echoes of Lorelei's words—*Carpe diem. Be bad.*—she'd been showered and changed and on her way before really thinking it all the way through. Her nerve had nearly failed her a dozen times on the short walk from her house to here, but now...

She couldn't regret the decision. She might not be able to say why she'd made that choice, but something about the feel of Connor's mouth on her neck, the caress of his hands under her jacket to the small of her back...it felt good. There was something liberating in this—more than just seizing the day. It was new and scary territory for her, but it felt right, too.

And it felt *good*. Connor's hands were truly talented, alternating between feather-light touches that sent shivers over her to strong caresses that left her knees weak. She might as well let go. It wasn't like Connor was a stranger, even if he wasn't what she'd call a friend. That strange place they inhabited with each other seemed perfect for exactly this.

It shouldn't make sense, but it sort of *did*. Vivi didn't care. Connor had answered the door shirtless, and the skin under her hands felt as good as it looked. The heat seeped through her jacket and shirt to warm her skin. She wanted more, though, not just warmth.

As if he was able to read her mind, Connor slid the zipper of her jacket down and pushed it off her shoulders. She felt her T-shirt rising until it stopped at her breasts. She lifted her arms as Connor broke their kiss long enough to sweep the shirt over her head. The cool rush of air over her skin was fleeting as Connor pulled her immediately back against his chest. The contact was shocking, yet Vivi wanted more, and she melted into him.

Her lips traced the ridge of muscle from his shoulder to his neck and Connor growled, the rumble vibrating through her from lips to toes. The world suddenly shifted, making her head spin, but Connor had carried her halfway down the hall before it fully registered, and a second later she felt cool sheets under her.

Connor loomed over her, those powerful arms bracketing her shoulders, holding him solid and steady, his eyes hot on her body and face. When he finally met her gaze she realized he was giving her one last chance to end this before it was too late.

She hooked a foot around his leg and slid it over his calf. She let her hands trace the planes of Connor's chest and felt the tightening of the muscles under her fingers. "It's already too late," she whispered.

The corner of Connor's mouth curved up. "But I've only just begun."

Her blood took his words as a promise, surging through her veins. And Connor made good on that promise, exploring every inch of her with unhurried, methodical intensity until she was whimpering and incoherent. She wanted to bring him to the same place, but her hands were fisted in the sheets as she tried to hang on to the last shreds of her sanity.

Not an inch of her skin went unmapped by his hands, then by his lips and tongue and teeth. He held her at the edge until she wanted to beg, but she couldn't find the words.

Connor was shaking, holding on to his control by mere strings in danger of breaking at any moment. Vivi felt like a flame under his hands—hot and alive and dangerous. Her responses were raw, honest and almost more than he could handle without combusting himself as well. She seemed designed expressly for him: her curves slotted perfectly against him, her skin responded to his touch, demanding more. Vivi's hands contained electricity. Her mouth... Her mouth did things to him that defied words.

The need to take her, lose himself in her, was overwhelming, and only the sting of Vivi's nails biting into his shoulders kept him grounded as he slid into her. Hot... Tight... Wet... The sensations fogged his brain.

Then Vivi was arching into him, pressing her hips hard against his, seeking more, searching for the rhythm. His hands fisted in her silky hair and Vivi scored tracks down his back. His mouth landed on hers as he quickened the pace, and he felt the tremors building until she broke.

The contractions and shudders of her orgasm pushed him over the edge himself, and the world dimmed at the edges.

He vaguely realized he'd shouted her name.

SEVEN

—

Vivi lay facedown in the bed. She hadn't moved other than to brush the hair out of her face since she'd rolled away from him. Her breathing had evened out and returned to normal, but beads of sweat still pooled in the indentation of her spine. Connor wasn't much for *was-it-good-for-you?* pillow talk, but Vivi's complete and continuing silence seemed odd. Finally she sighed and rolled to her side to face him. Her brow was furrowed slightly.

"Deep thoughts, Vivi?"

"I'm not really capable of higher brain functions yet."

He'd take that as a compliment, but he was in a similar state. "That explains your silence."

"Actually, that just seemed..." She laughed quietly. "Prudent."

"Prudent?"

"It's an awkward enough situation, and we're not real good at talking without it denigrating into something else at the best of times. I'm not keen on the idea of arguing with you while I'm naked."

"You do have a point."

That earned him a smile. "Plus, it would kind of kill the afterglow, you know?"

"Well, I kind of suck at the afterglow chitchat anyway."

"See? Silence seemed the best bet."

"I think I'm slightly offended," he teased.

"Why?"

"Sex but no talking? Just using me for my body?"

"The tables may have turned, but you have to have more experience in this situation. And you just said you suck at the chitchat anyway."

He tried to keep his voice light. "It doesn't mean that I'm happy to be your boy toy for the night."

Vivi rolled her eyes. "Don't pretend you're that fragile."

"I'm a musician. I'm artistic and sensitive, you know."

She snorted. "I work with artists every day. I'm not likely to swallow that line."

"You're a hard woman, Vivi." He rubbed a hand over his face.

"I try." She smiled at him.

"That wasn't a compliment."

"Coming from you? Of course not. But I'm going to take it as one anyway."

The relaxed mood evaporated and he felt the usual tension building. It was at odds with the lingering scents of sex and sweat. "Because you want to be a hard-ass?"

Vivi pushed to a seated position and dragged the sheet up to cover her breasts. "Boy, you really do suck at this part."

"Maybe we should have stuck with the silence." His languorous, sated mood was giving way to a headache. He dropped his head back onto the pillow and draped an arm over his eyes. Vivi equaled trouble. Always.

"I tried to tell you."

"But what you haven't told me is why."

"I just did. I don't want to fight, so talking—"

"I get that." He levered himself up onto his elbows. "Why are you even here? Your feelings toward me are pretty clear, so why on earth are you in my bed?"

Vivi was quiet for a moment. "I could ask you something similar."

His pride answered for him. "What kind of man turns down sex?"

"What kind of man accepts sex from a woman he doesn't like?" she shot back.

"What kind of woman offers sex to a man she hates?"

The sharp intake of breath told him he'd hit the mark. Vivi's jaw tightened. "I knew I shouldn't have come. I should have just stayed in a cold shower until the urge passed. Or should've just kept drinking until I forgot."

"As someone who was doing both of those things when you showed up..."

She held up a hand. "Maybe now's a good time for me to leave." She edged toward end of the bed, pulling the sheet with her as she went. "I'd say to just forget this ever happened, but I'll settle for you not bringing it up in public."

"Ashamed of yourself, Vivi?"

He caught the stiffening of her shoulders, the telltale flush of pink across the tops of her breasts. She shot him a dirty look and that supercilious eyebrow went up again. "Well, aligning myself with thousands of other groupies isn't something I'm going to put on my résumé, you know."

Argh. "What is this obsession you have with groupies?"

"Because I've seen you charm people and I prided myself on being immune to it. And then..." She swung her legs off the bed and stood, seemingly unaware or uncaring of the fact she was gloriously naked.

"Then what?"

"Then I spent time with you this week, and I started to think that maybe I wasn't completely right about you. That you'd changed or matured. I fell for it— again—and I shouldn't have." Vivi squatted, sorting through the piles of discarded clothing. "I'm going to kill Lorelei," she muttered.

That was a bit of a non sequitur. "I'm afraid to ask what Lorelei has to do with any of this."

"Nothing. This was a mistake. I shouldn't have come, so I'll just go. I'm really sorry." Her words degraded into mumbles, but he could pick up the occasional "stupid" and "insane." He couldn't be sure which one of them she was referring to.

She was right, though. They should just forget this ever happened. But he didn't want her to leave. Even though she infuriated him, his body was still primed for her touch. The edge was off, but the need was still there. How had they gotten to this point?

"Vivi, wait."

"What?"

Vivi had swallowed her pride to come here; he not only appreciated that, he understood how much it had cost her. He should—and could—offer her something in return. He crossed the space and captured her face between his hands. Her eyes widened as he leaned in and kissed her.

"I've wanted to do that since eighth grade."

"You're kidding me."

"Nope."

"Then why didn't you?"

"Because I didn't want my bleeding head handed back to me."

Vivi's lips twitched at the image.

"I've never been a glutton for abuse."

"You like to hand it out, though. At least to me."

"I could say the same about you."

That statement sent Vivi's eyebrows to her hairline, and he knew once she recovered from the shock she'd be back at his throat again. Right now he really just wanted her to come back to bed.

"I asked you for a truce earlier tonight, and it was a serious offer." *Especially now.*

"Forgive and forget? Bygones and all that?"

"The apology was also sincere. Why don't we just decide that the statute of limitations for childhood and teenage idiocy has expired and go forth acting like grownups."

"That sounds very mature." Her lips twitched. "It might be a hard habit to break, though."

"Any current idiocy can still be game. Just not old grudges."

The last of the hostility drained out of her. "I think I can agree to that."

"Glad to hear it."

Vivi looked at the clothes she held in her hands. "Now I don't know what to do."

He took the shirt she was holding and dropped it to the floor. "I'd like it if you stayed."

He sounded like the lyrics to one of his songs. It was embarrassing, but Vivi's cautious "Really?" made it worthwhile. It was a strange feeling—one he didn't understand or care to explore right now, though. His body was already recovering, simply from being this close to her.

"Eighth grade, remember?"

Vivi's smile was seductive. She stepped closer and placed a hand on his chest. The smile got bigger as she looked up at him. "You had braces in eighth grade."

"So did you."

"At least we won't have to worry about getting them locked together."

The clock beside the bed ticked closer to four. Connor was snoring softly beside her, one arm thrown over her stomach, but Vivi couldn't sleep. She was sated and exhausted; every muscle in her body felt like pudding, but her brain just wouldn't turn off and let her sleep. Not that her brain was working properly by any stretch of the imagination; it jumped from topic to topic like a flea on speed, unable to process any thoughts beyond the superficial and not following any kind of logical progression.

It was frustrating, but it was probably self-defense. Thinking too much about the last week—much less the last few hours—might cause her head to explode.

She eased out from under Connor's arm. He rolled over but didn't wake up, and she exhaled in relief. Her clothes were still a tangled mess, so she grabbed one of Connor's shirts hanging off a chairback and slipped it on. The scent of Connor's aftershave drifted up as she buttoned it.

On tiptoes, she crept into the living room. She knew the apartment well; Gabe Morrow had bought all of the art on the walls from her gallery and she'd been here many times, delivering or helping to hang. Although Connor was a temporary tenant, he'd made himself at home and his things were scattered throughout the room—it wasn't untidy, but it showed Connor was comfortable here.

But there was nothing personal—no photos or anything like that. It underscored the fact that she didn't really know much about the man Connor was now. And it also reminded her that his stay was temporary. *That* made all of this a little easier to understand, at least.

The biggest change to the apartment was the baby grand piano that now sat close to the balcony doors. Had Connor had one brought in for himself? To the best of her knowledge Gabe didn't play, but that didn't mean he hadn't decided to get a piano anyway. It would make sense that Connor would want or need a piano in whatever accommodations he took, but now that she knew he was nursing an injury, having a piano here seemed like it would be a temptation or a distraction.

She smoothed a hand over the lacquered lid. Connor's parents had a piano in the front parlor—an old upright that half the kids in the neighborhood had banged on until Connor discovered his passion and put it off-limits so they didn't knock it out of tune. Even she'd tinkered on the keys as a child while her mother and Mrs. Mansfield had coffee in another room. As she'd gotten older, she'd been able to sit in her room and hear Connor practicing next door, mastering everything from Chopin to Count Basie to Billy Joel.

She sat on the bench and ran her hands lightly over the keys without making a sound. She traced the shapes and the edges with her fingers, not really wanting to think about the repercussions of what she'd just done, but unable to escape it.

Against all good judgment she'd let her libido bring her here tonight, and that had worked out pretty well, making her now question her judgment in general. Letting go of all that adolescent angst was an excellent idea—in theory, at least. It was a shame, though, that she hadn't done that *before* she'd shown up at his door like she was desperate for his body.

Did she feel better? Definitely. Lorelei might have had a point about the joys of being bad after all. All the tension seemed gone from her body, if not her mind. If this was what being bad was all about, she now understood the appeal. How something could feel right and wrong at the same time, though, was a conundrum her brain just couldn't process. Had she used him? Had he used her? Was it really possible that years of angst and anger could disappear just like that? Was she being shallow, falling under the allure of Connor Mansfield? No, that much she was sure of. Whatever she'd done, whatever this was, it had nothing to do with who Connor was other than just himself.

Like that hadn't proved tempting enough.

But why had it happened *now* instead of five or ten years ago?

Maybe things just had their own timelines, and she shouldn't question it. Tonight felt momentous—and not just because of the toe-curling experiences she'd discovered in Connor's bed. No, she felt on the edge of something—like she'd left a part of herself behind and was moving into something new.

But that something new wouldn't—couldn't—involve Connor. He wasn't a permanent kind of guy.

How many women had Connor made the papers with? It was a veritable *Who's Who* of celebrity singles—all of them beautiful, powerful and talented—but none of them had lasted longer than a month or so. The idea of a fling had never appealed to her, though; it just wasn't something she thought she'd do. Now she seemed to be in one, and while she didn't quite understand it, she was okay with it. Connor might not be a permanent kind of guy, but he seemed to bring about excellent transitions.

Vivi felt more than heard Connor behind her, and a second later she felt his hands stroking her hair. Leaning back, she let her weight rest against Connor's thighs as he ran those long fingers through her hair, removing the tangles. She wanted to purr. Obviously her libido wasn't done with her yet.

"Do you play, Vivi?"

She shook her head. "Just 'Chopsticks.' Badly, I might add."

Connor scooted her forward on the bench and moved in behind her, his chest pressed against her back, his naked thighs surrounding hers. The muscles in those thighs felt like iron and the crisp hairs tickled her skin. His hands slid under hers, lining them up from fingers to elbows as he began to play slowly.

"I thought you were supposed to be resting your hands."

"Shh." His breath moved the hair at her temple.

It was a simple but beautiful string of notes, and as long as she remained still and relaxed, her hands moved with his.

And now that she knew exactly how talented Connor's hands were, watching him play seemed intensely erotic, and feeling him play under her hands made it all the more intimate.

Too intimate. Too intense.

She let her hands slide off his and into her lap.

Connor's fingers changed direction and tempo, and the string of notes turned into a melody. The muscles in his forearms flexed, and she could feel his chest and shoulders moving against her like a massage.

And then he began to sing quietly, his voice just inches above her ear.

Oh, it's raining,
Outside her window, inside her soul.

His voice. *Mercy*. It was a shot of straight sex, but served with a side of emotion that reverberated through her. She let her hands slide over the thick muscle of his thighs and heard the quick catch of his breath.

And her blue eyes,
Just keep cryin',
While she remembers a love untold.

The music died abruptly when Connor's hands came to rest on hers again, twining their fingers together and tracing them along the seams where his thighs met hers.

"I'm not familiar with that song."

Connor's chin rested on her shoulder and his breath moved across her neck. "It's just something I've been working on."

"It's beautiful."

She felt his shrug. "It's different. We'll see how it goes over."

"It'll be a hit. Just like the others."

"That's the hope."

"Hope? You're Connor freakin' Mansfield."

"The public is fickle. That's why there are so many one-hit wonders."

He released her hands. One arm snaked around her waist, his thumb brushing lightly over the bottom of her ribs. The other went back to the keyboard where he started to play again, soft and slow. She recognized the top-line melody of one of his early songs.

"You never know when they'll turn on you."

Connor sounded...almost vulnerable. Worried. That was ridiculous. Why would he be? Or had the sordid and tawdry headlines affected him more than he allowed others to know? "Your fans love you."

"They love an idea. An image. That Connor has little to do with me personally."

"And who's that Connor?" She was almost afraid to ask, but the quiet and the dark created an intimacy of the moment that lent itself to deep questions.

She felt his smile against her cheek. "Interestingly enough, I'd say it was the same Connor you dislike so much."

That didn't make sense. The arrogance, the swagger, the lady-killing charm. The confidence... She, too, had been reacting to that—negatively, of course—but now that they'd called their truce she was realizing and remembering everything else she knew about Connor. How kind he'd been to Lorelei when she was deep in her crush on him years ago. How serious he was about this competition—and not just to beat her. She thought shamefully about some of her own motivations. How hard he'd practiced, even amid the taunts of boys more interested in touchdowns than Tchaikovsky. How ready he'd been to put the past behind them.

Had she been judging him unfairly? Using her own adolescent grudges and his recent notoriety to prevent her from seeing Connor as a person?

Connor was far more complex than she'd realized or given him credit for. Consciously at least. The fact none of this surprised her meant she'd known it all along and just refused to recognize it. Wow, she *was* shallow.

No. Everything had been such a roller coaster since that closet door slammed shut, and in retrospect she'd gotten glimpses into Connor that had led her here tonight. *Great.* That just made tonight even more complicated. Maybe her subconscious was smarter than she gave it credit and that was why it had let her libido push her here. To force her to think. Damn it, she didn't want to think. Wasn't not thinking the whole point of *carpe diem*?

Vivi put her right hand on the keyboard and tried to remember the notes Connor had played earlier. As she stumbled around Connor began pointing to the correct keys. After a few tries she had sixteen counts' worth.

"Just repeat that phrase. Same tempo."

Connor's left hand began a much more complicated set, playing perfectly off her few notes, yet it was completely different than the earlier tune. It was incredible not only to witness but to be a part of. She played the last note, and Connor ended with a flourish.

She dropped her hands back into her lap and, surprisingly, Connor's followed. He ran his fingers gently over her wrists and arms.

"That's amazing, Connor." She felt him shrug in response. "I mean it. I felt like I was actually playing something."

"You were."

"With help, though."

"That doesn't mean you weren't part of it."

But Connor was a solo act. Still, there was something wonderful about being inside his arms as he

played. The sensation of feeling him create the music...
It was silly, but she wanted him to play something else.
She was about to ask when she remembered he was
supposed to be resting his hands.

There was a slight pang of disappointment, but it
was quickly routed when Connor placed a feather-light
kiss on her neck. His hands moved from her arms to
the buttons of her borrowed shirt, opening them and
sliding inside to caress her lower stomach and tease
her breasts. His movements became more focused, his
thumb rasping across her nipple, wringing a gasp from
her and causing her to grip his thighs for purchase.
Vivi could feel his erection hardening against her back,
and her breath picked up as his did. She arched, pressing her breast into his hand when a finger slipped between her legs and slid inside.

Just like that the switch was flipped, and Vivi's
focus narrowed sharply. She opened her legs wider,
quietly demanding more, and Connor obliged, whis-
pering encouragement between pressing hot kisses
against her neck and shoulders.

With a groan, Connor turned her around, wrapping
her legs around his waist, and leaned her back against
the piano. Her elbows hit the keyboard, making an off-
key chord, as Connor flicked the rest of the buttons out
of their holes and spread the edges of her shirt wide.

A big hand slid up her torso, over her chest and
neck, before circling around her nape to tangle in her
hair. His eyes were hooded as he examined the freckles
sprinkled across the tops of her breasts. A tug pulled
her fully into his lap again, where the crisp hairs on
his chest tickled her nipples as his mouth claimed hers.

A surge of those powerful thighs had him on his feet, and Vivi clung to him as he carried her back to the bedroom and collapsed onto the bed.

She had no idea what she was doing. It scared her not to know what this was. But it didn't scare her enough to stop, because whatever this was, it was good. She'd sort out the rest later.

Connor had vague memories of Vivi kissing him as the first weak rays of sunshine began to lighten the curtains. He didn't realize it had been a goodbye kiss until the alarm went off and he woke to find her side of the bed empty and cold. He wasn't quite sure what to make of her sneaky departure, but since their first attempt at post-coital conversation had ended in her nearly walking out, he was almost relieved not to have to deal with the possible awkwardness this morning.

Almost.

Two hours later, he was seated between the director of the local humanities council and the director of an after-school program at a brunch meeting of the city's non-profit organizations. His mom was seated across from him, but she was there in her capacity as the current chair of...something. He couldn't remember which of the many organizations she was involved with. The broader purpose of the meeting was to discuss fundraising in general, but half the people in the room had known him since he was a child, which made this a little surreal, to say the least.

Vivi was about five chairs down, and other than a very quick greeting when she hadn't quite met his eyes, they hadn't spoken two words to each other. Everyone seemed very careful to keep them apart and refrained from talking to him about Vivi—which only took this to new levels of surrealism, because that *never* happened. But every now and then he heard someone say her name or heard her laugh. This was Vivi's element; she knew every single person here—as a contributing adult, unlike him—and she had probably worked with most of them at some point.

He might have been imagining it, but Vivi seemed to be avoiding him even more than usual. Either she was overcompensating, so as not to give away their activities of the previous evening, or she was having serious regrets. Either way, it irked him.

He kept half an eye on her, noting how she kept stifling yawns as the meal concluded. Once the mingling began, he eventually ended up close enough to actually speak to her—except that there were seven other people standing with them. Vivi looked distinctly uncomfortable, and she'd probably bolt if given the opportunity. She still wouldn't meet his eyes, and he was seconds from pulling her aside and finding out what the problem was.

But Dr. Robins, the head of an inner-city free clinic, put a stop to that plan. "So, how was last night?"

It took Connor a second to figure out what the man was talking about. Damn, the jazz cruise seemed like it had happened *days* ago. "It was very nice. I haven't done one of those riverboat cruises in years." Seeing his opening, he turned to Vivi. "What about you? Did you enjoy yourself last night, Vivi?"

The mimosa in Vivi's hand sloshed dangerously close to the rim as she jumped, but she recovered quickly. She shot him a warning look. "I did, thank you. Very much." Then the corner of her mouth twitched. "It's funny. I wasn't sure that I would, but I was very pleasantly surprised."

It was very hard to keep his amusement in check and his face neutral. "Glad to hear it. You left so quickly once we docked I wasn't sure."

"I was tired and wanted to get home. Plus, I didn't want Lorelei to wonder where I was."

That made sense. Since none of the people around them understood the subtext, he decided to push a little harder. "It was quite a busy evening, wasn't it? So many different things happening. What was your favorite part, Vivi?"

Her cheeks turned a little pink. "There's so much to choose from. But you're quite good on the piano, and I found myself enjoying that more than I thought I would."

He was going to ask her something else, but a woman he didn't know spoke first.

"You played for the guests last night? How wonderful for them."

Great. Vivi shot him a smile that told him she'd done that on purpose. "Just a couple of songs to help the party along."

"There's a piano here. Maybe you could play for us?"

Vivi answered before he could. "He can't." All eyes swiveled in her direction.

She wouldn't. "Vivi..."

"It's not fair, Connor." Her voice took on that clipped, chilly tone he knew so well. "You have this great talent, and it makes me look me look bad when you keep showing off like that." She turned to the crowd. "I'm doing everything I can to keep up as it is. He has an unfair advantage, you know. Don't encourage him."

He wanted to kiss her. She could have let him try to get out of it himself, but she hadn't. Vivi was actually watching his back. An unfamiliar feeling spread through his chest, and as the conversation turned, he smiled his thanks at Vivi. She nodded.

Vivi was pulled away a moment later by her mother, and when the event finally broke up a little while later, Vivi was nowhere in sight. That irritated feeling returned. Could he have misread or misunderstood something? He didn't like that idea.

"Mr. Mansfield?"

Connor turned to find a pretty hostess flashing a flirtatious smile at him.

"You had a phone call earlier. A Miss White left a number for you to return her call." She handed him a piece of paper and her brow wrinkled in confusion. "It's strange. I think she said it was about piano lessons, but that just seems crazy considering...well, who you are."

Heat rushed to his groin at the mention of "piano lessons." "Thanks. It makes sense to me."

He put his mother into a cab in almost unseemly haste, and started walking the six blocks back to the Quarter, dialing as he walked. Vivi answered on the second ring.

"You are terrible, Connor Mansfield."

"Where are you?"

"The gallery. I couldn't stay at the brunch. Between Madeline Jensen's upset that I wouldn't let you play and the fact you seemed to be doing your best to embarrass me..."

"That's what you get for sneaking out before I woke up."

"I was hoping it would be less awkward that way."

Vivi didn't seem to be feeling that awkwardness now. "And avoiding me?"

"Self-preservation."

"You are hell on the ego, Vivi."

"I think your ego can handle it. So..." She trailed off, and the silence was so complete he wondered if the call had been dropped. Then he heard her clear her throat. "So what happens now?"

The awkwardness was back. He'd never heard her sound so hesitant. "I thought you wanted piano lessons."

There was another of those long silences, and Connor wondered if he'd said the wrong thing. Then he heard her laugh softly.

"Yeah. I think I'd like that."

EIGHT

—

At the one-week mark he and Vivi had been running neck-and-neck in the fundraising. Well, once he counted his matching her funds plan, at least. Early in week two Vivi had pulled ahead by landing a couple of corporate sponsors on her side, but one message on Twitter pulled him back into the lead. That trick had earned him an earful from Vivi, but Vivi's tongue had lost a bit of its sting these days.

In a way he missed the battle of wills and wits, but while the tone had changed, Vivi still kept him on his toes. She was the first to call him on things, but also the first to give credit and accolades. She could be hell on his ego when she took him down a peg, but things were different now.

When it came to the actual challenges, like today's work for the food bank, Vivi was definitely kicking his butt. She could organize people like a pro, and her team always ran with easy efficiency while he looked like he was trying to herd cats.

It was almost embarrassing, but he could take it.

Everyone had their strengths and areas of expertise, and no one could touch Vivi when it came to any aspect of volunteer work.

Two weeks ago he would have had something snarky to say about that, but now... He didn't have to admit to grudging admiration for Vivi's talents. He could just be impressed by them. Vivi was completely focused and no-nonsense, but she had a way of getting work and money out of people and leaving them thinking it was all their idea.

Now, *that* was a talent. And, as he was discovering, Vivi had many interesting talents.

After that initial awkwardness the day after, Vivi had slowly warmed to the new status quo. She wasn't openly advertising that change, but even the bloggers had picked up on what they called an "easing of hostilities."

If they only knew...

Connor felt better than he had in months. He might not be getting a lot of sleep, thanks to Vivi, but otherwise he was feeling grounded and sane and normal—and that probably had something to do with Vivi as well. It should feel stranger than it did, and that was strange in and of itself.

He caught Vivi's eye across the room, and she gave him a half-smile before looking at his untidy piles of unfinished work and raising her eyebrows. "How's it going over there?" she called.

"Perfectly."

She shook her head. "Doesn't look like it."

"It's like walking into the middle of major surgery. It looks like a bloody mess, but it's all under control."

"Glad to hear it. I just hope you get it finished today."

So did he. However, it might end up like their workday in the Lower Ninth Ward where Vivi's team had finally had to come help his under the mercy rule. He turned around and gave a few encouraging shouts to his Imps and was gratified to see them pick up the pace. Then he jumped a pile of canned green beans and walked over to her.

"How do you manage it?"

"They're kids. They need clear, specific instructions." She dropped her chin and gave him a look that would have done the nuns in high school proud. "And a good example to follow, I might add."

"Hey, I'm working my butt off over there."

Vivi just shrugged. "After we're finished here I'll send a few of the Cherubim over to help."

"Much appreciated."

"Well, y'all will be here until midnight if I don't."

"We definitely don't want that." At her look, he dropped his voice and added, "I was kind of planning on taking you to dinner tonight. I got reservations at LaSalle."

Vivi looked suitably impressed. "LaSalle is booked out for months."

"Fame has its perks. Table reservations is just one of them."

Vivi looked uncomfortable. "Isn't that rather public?"

"It's less public than this." He pointed to the cameras and the crowds.

"This is different."

"Ashamed to be seen with me or something?" he challenged.

"No, that's not it. I just didn't know that we…it… *that*…was for public knowledge. I thought we were staying low, under the radar."

Ah. "You like sneaking around?" He liked her discretion. It was a nice change from the view-all, tell-all of celebrity relationships. Or maybe Vivi had a streak in her he didn't know about that enjoyed the game. He could get behind that, too.

"That's not it either. It's just…" She trailed off and frowned.

"It's just…?" he prompted.

Vivi sighed and shrugged. "Dinner sounds great. What time?"

"Seven. I'll pick you up."

"No, I'll meet you at your place." At his look, she added, "I need to run by the gallery, so I'll do that on my way." She added a smile. "I'll see you at seven."

She went back to work, leaving him feeling a little off-kilter. Vivi wasn't like any other woman he'd ever met, that was for sure. He was quickly discovering, however, that that wasn't a bad thing. It sounded cheesy, but Vivi brought out the Boy Scout in him. He found himself wanting to do the smaller things, like pick her up for dinner. It didn't make sense. He snorted. When had Vivi ever made sense to him?

Connor turned around, fully intending to get this job finished as soon as possible, and he saw his Imps standing idle, watching him. "Who called a union break? They're killing us here."

Before he could get anything accomplished, though,

his phone rang. A glance at the number had him sighing. He really didn't want to wade back into the fray today. He was enjoying the interlude from his life.

Balancing the phone uncomfortably on his shoulder, he closed a box and strapped tape across the top. "What's up, Angie?"

"I've got excellent news."

His agent wasn't one to exaggerate, so whatever it was it had to be damn good. "I like excellent news."

"In light of the paternity test results, the plaintiff's countersuit has been dismissed and we have our permanent injunction."

"And in simple English that means...?"

"Katy Arras has been told to shut her lying trap."

"That *is* excellent news."

"Thought you might like that. In other good news, thanks to your current charity work and some internet search engine magic I don't understand, all that dirt is now buried on page two and beyond. It's pretty much over."

The dirt would never be completely washed away, but he'd settle for it being lost on the internet. He might be personally vindicated, but people would still mutter about the rumors behind his back, wondering how much was really true. Those kinds of stories stuck around forever, becoming urban legends and the butt of jokes.

At least he wasn't the first. He was in company with some of the greats. "You are a doll, Angie"

"That's why you pay me the big bucks. How are you holding up down there?"

"I'm home, not exiled to Siberia."

Angie, who considered the suburbs too rustic to visit and New York the only city outside California worth acknowledging, snorted. "Well, keep hanging in there. You're getting all kinds of good press."

"And I'm having a good time, too."

"Good for you. Just don't have *too* good of a time. One Katy Arras a year is my limit."

"Don't worry. I'm being a good boy."

That caused Angie to chuckle. "Well, don't take that too far either," she warned. "Remember your brand."

"How could I forget it?" He didn't bother to hide his exasperation, but Angie ignored it.

"I'll be in touch next week. I've got some plans cooking for March and April. When are you planning to go back into the studio?"

"Don't know yet. The brain is still recovering from the tour." Angie didn't know about his hands, and he saw no reason to go into that now. She was still reeling from hearing about all of his plans that didn't involve going back into the studio.

"Keep me posted."

"I will. Right now I have boxes to pack."

"Oh, yeah, that charity stuff. Good for you. Keep it up."

He could almost hear the dismissive wave. Beyond the PR op, Angie didn't have much use for this, and that irked him as well. He snorted. He really was finding his inner Boy Scout.

"By the way, I'm coming down there for Mardi Gras," she added.

"Good luck finding a hotel room."

"I can't just stay with you?" she teased.

That would make things very awkward with Vivi. "In a word, no. In two words, hell no. I like my privacy."

"That's typical of you. Fine," she huffed. "I'll make some calls. I do know other people."

"I'll be happy to point you in the right direction for whatever you want to do once you're here," he offered.

"That I'll take you up on. Talk to you later. 'Bye."

Connor stuck his phone back in his pocket. He didn't really want to think about March or April or going back into the studio. He'd given Angie unfettered access to his schedule for the last six years, and while he appreciated her efforts on his behalf, he'd made them both enough money for him to take a little control back. Of his name, his time, his image and his freakin' *brand*.

He wasn't ignorant of the fact that this new desire for control and his current frustration with the status quo were probably fueling his situation with Vivi. It wasn't just lust—although that did help, he thought with a small smile—it was a whole new approach to his life. The solid confirmation of that knowledge sent a mini-shockwave through him. He hadn't known he had it in him.

How novel. *I'm growing as a person*. Vivi would have quite a bit of fun with that. In fact he might have to mention it, just to see what she'd have to say about it.

True to her word, Vivi and her crew came over to help his team finish up—but true to her nature she waited until they'd conceded defeat and the points were added to her column before she did. And when she shot him a smile full of secret promise Connor was very glad he'd come home.

All of his choices seemed to be working out quite well.

Vivi slid her feet into her shoes and opened her bedroom door. Lorelei stood against the wall, facing her door, arms crossed over her chest. "Spill."

"Excuse me?"

"I've kept my mouth shut all week long about your late nights and lack of details—"

"And it's been bliss." Vivi stepped past her, but Lorelei ignored the hint and followed her into the living room. This wasn't exactly how she'd planned to tell Lorelei about the rather dramatic shift in her life, but Lorelei hadn't been home much and time had gotten away from her.

"But now you're all dressed up. Your new snuggle monkey is finally taking you out on the town, huh?"

She raised an eyebrow at Lorelei. *"Snuggle monkey?"*

"It wasn't my first choice of term, but the others were more vulgar and would have gotten you mad at me. I know you're having sex, and I'm dying to know who with."

"Like *that's* any of your business."

"No, I think it's great. You're all glowy and relaxed. Not only are you having sex, you're having some *awesome* sex."

Vivi couldn't stop the blush. She tried to hide it by turning away, but Lorelei saw and pounced.

"Whoa! *That* good, huh? I have to know the identity of this sex god."

This was not exactly how she'd pictured this conversation. Vivi searched for words, but Lorelei took it as hesitation.

"If he's taking you out tonight, it's not exactly a secret affair, you know." She paused and her eyes narrowed. "Oh, God, unless... He's not married or anything, is he?"

"For heaven's sake, Lorelei, of course not."

"Well, it *would* explain all the secrecy."

Vivi took a deep breath. "I'm going out with Connor."

"Connor who?"

"Mansfield. How many other Connors do you know?"

Lorelei looked disappointed. "Well, I read that all wrong. I didn't realize you had a Saints and Sinners thing tonight."

"I don't."

"Then why are you going to dinner with Connor?"

Either Lorelei was very dense, or this news really was too incredible to believe. "Because he asked me to."

Lorelei's eyebrows knitted together. "This makes no sense. My world is officially askew. You're not planning on dumping his meal in his lap, are you?"

"It's not on the agenda, no. And I'd never make a scene like that at LaSalle."

"LaSalle? *Wow.* Hang on. All these late nights and now..." The furrow on her brow deepened, then her eyes grew wide in shock. "Wait. *Connor* is your secret snuggle monkey?"

Oh, Lord. "Lorelei..."

Lorelei rose to her feet, blinking and shaking her head. "You're sleeping with *Connor*?"

"Lorelei..."

Her voice rose to a shout. "You're having *sex* with Connor Mansfield?"

"Let's not announce that to the entire neighborhood, please."

"Oh, my God, you *are* sleeping with him. Oh. My. *God. When* did this start? How? Why? I need lots of details."

Vivi didn't feel like sharing details at the moment, and she certainly didn't have good answers to *how* or *why*. It made her head hurt to make sense of it. This was new territory, and it kind of freaked her out when she thought about it too much.

She made a point of looking at her watch and picking up her purse. "I've got to run."

Lorelei snatched her purse out of her hand. "Oh, no, you don't. You're not dropping a bomb like that and then prancing out of here like it's nothing."

"Give me my purse."

"Give me some answers."

"This is not your business. I don't owe you any answers about anything."

"I've spent my entire life listening to you complain about Connor and how he makes your existence miserable—so, yeah, you do owe me some answers now."

Oh, how she wished she had answers to give. "Connor and I have...um...resolved many of our differences—"

"I should certainly hope so."

Argh. "And we are...um...moving past old grudges and...um...moving forward as adults."

"By knocking boots."

"Must you be so crude?" Lorelei made it sound tawdry. Maybe it was. Vivi just didn't want to think so.

"I don't see you denying it."

"Fine." She lowered her voice to a whisper, even though she was in the privacy of her own house. "Yes, I am sleeping with Connor. We are adults, and it's nobody else's business..."

Lorelei stomped back to the couch, dragging Vivi with her, and forced her to sit. "First—congratulations. I mean, *Connor.* Yum." She fanned her face. "But we'll come back to that in a minute. You keep saying it's nobody's business—and that's sort of true—but the minute you're spotted with Connor at LaSalle—and you *will* be spotted—it will be *everyone's* business."

"The media has left Connor alone recently."

"It's not the press you need to worry about. It's everyone with a cell phone who wants to make a quick buck. You'll be on all the blogs before midnight, I guarantee it. Even if you weren't sleeping together—and I do intend to come back to that, so don't think you're going to weasel out—the world will think you are."

"Well, I can't control what people think."

"But you'll certainly care once it's your name being bandied about. And after all the recent gossip about Connor's, *ahem,* preferences..."

"Which you never claimed to believe in the first place."

"I'm not Jane Q. Public in middle America, with no reason not to believe it."

"I'm not worried about middle America. Most of them think New Orleans is a den of iniquity anyway. I'm not running for political office or competing for Miss America, so I don't care what Jane Q. Public thinks about anything. The only people whose opinions I care about know me—and Connor, too, for that matter—so it's not likely they'll get caught up in any gossip frenzy."

"Good for you, Vivi." There was genuine pride in Lorelei's voice. "I just hope it's worth it."

"It is," she answered without thinking, and as Lorelei's eyes lit up Vivi desperately wanted to suck the words back in.

"*Now* we're getting somewhere. Exactly *how* worth it is it?"

Damn it, she could feel the heat in her face again.

Lorelei sighed. "You are one lucky girl."

Silently, she agreed—and that shocked her a little.

"So what happened? What changed?"

"I don't really know. We were spending all this time together, and actually talking to him kind of made me see things—him—differently, and..." She shrugged. "*Carpe diem,* I guess."

"Wow. Just *wow.*" Lorelei leaned forward. "So is this serious? Like going somewhere?"

Vivi nearly choked. "Oh, no—no, no. It's just casual."

"And you're okay with that?" Lorelei was wide-eyed with shock.

She had to think about it, and that kind of shocked her, too. "Yeah. I think I am."

"I gotta say, Vivi, I never would have expected this."

"Me neither."

Lorelei handed over her purse. "Then enjoy it. Every single minute of it. You deserve it."

"Thanks, sweetie." The grandfather clock began to bong the hour. She was late. "I've got to go. Don't wait up, okay?"

"Since I know you won't dish the details, I guess I won't. By the way—how does it feel?"

Vivi was shrugging into her coat. "How does what feel?"

"Being the bad one, for once."

Was she being bad? Not really. Reckless? Maybe. Less than circumspect? Definitely. But she was an adult; Connor was an adult. She might be being a little bit bad, but in comparison to others, Vivi was still on the narrow path. "I have to admit that it feels pretty darn good."

"Told ya so."

Dressed as she was, it was a little too chilly to be walking, and her shoes weren't exactly designed for navigating the cobblestones and often ankle-twisting sidewalks of the French Quarter. It would take longer to drive than walk to Connor's place, but that couldn't be helped. And if she left her car on Connor's block, he wouldn't have to take her home in the middle of the night either. Although she'd spent her entire life in this city, and the blocks between Royal Street and Washington Square were far from deserted or particularly dangerous, Connor had developed a chivalrous streak that refused to let her walk home alone in the wee hours of the morning.

She'd lied when she'd said she had to go by the gallery first. She'd told herself that she didn't want to give Lorelei a chance to embarrass her in front of Connor, but that wasn't entirely true. She needed to keep things very separate in her mind, for her sanity's sake, and Connor picking her up like this was an actual date would blur those lines.

But this *was* an actual date, her inner voice reminded her. A very public one. And the thought of "dating" Connor opened up a whole new slew of thoughts she wasn't really willing to process. *No,* she told herself. Going public didn't change the nature of this. Connor was temporary. A change from the norm. A transition from the old Vivi to the new Vivi.

Right.

Connor buzzed her up, and the sight that greeted her caused her to wobble on her stilettos. *Mercy.* She was accustomed to his bad-boy rocker look, and she'd gotten used to the more casual look he'd been sporting during Saints and Sinners, but this... Connor was downright devastating in black pants, white button-down shirt and a blazer. It was completely simple, but something about it just flipped every switch in her body. This wasn't Connor the Rock Star, Connor the Sinner, or even Connor Her Arch Enemy; this was Connor the Man, all strength and assurance and everything the Y chromosome had to brag about.

"You're gorgeous, Vivi."

His compliment shook her out of her shock. A quick inventory told her she wasn't staring openmouthed or drooling. "You look pretty darn good yourself."

An eyebrow arched up. "We better go quickly, then."

"What? Why?"

"You look good enough to eat in small, slow bites, and we'll never make our reservation if I indulge."

The words carried promise and warning, and they nearly caused her to wobble again. Who cared about their reservation? Who needed food anyway? *This*, though...

She took a step forward.

The buzz of the intercom stopped her.

"That's our taxi." Connor opened the door for her and waited, but her feet didn't want to move. "You ready?"

No. "Sure."

The cab driver did a double-take when he saw Connor, and then spent much of the trip with one eye on the rearview mirror. Connor just shrugged good-naturedly and thanked the cabbie when he got effusive over Connor's music. Vivi knew it was a normal occurrence, and tried not to let it bother her that she couldn't talk to her date because the cabbie was. Connor apologized with a smile and a squeeze of her knee. And when the driver asked for a picture with Connor to add to his collection of celebrities he'd driven, Vivi got to play photographer.

Connor's life was different, that was for sure.

It wasn't until the taxi pulled away that Vivi realized she'd been so distracted that she hadn't realized where they were. "LaSalle is three blocks that way."

"I know. I wanted to show you this first."

Vivi looked around. She knew exactly where she was—Julia Street in the Warehouse District—but she didn't see anything out of the ordinary. Connor was pointing at an old three-story coffee warehouse that hadn't benefited yet from the revival of the neighborhood. "What am I looking at?"

"My new building." He held up a key ring. "I closed this afternoon, after I left the food bank." Connor unlocked the door and it swung open on rusty protesting hinges.

Vivi followed him inside, and Connor flipped on the light. The inside was as dilapidated as the outside, but the exposed brick walls and hardwood floors held promise of future beauty. It was a huge space, and their footsteps echoed.

"What do you need a warehouse for?"

Connor's grin spread from ear to ear. "This is the future home of ConMan Records."

He seemed to think she'd have a clue what that meant, but whatever it was he was proud and excited about it. The enthusiasm was contagious. "I'm not entirely sure what that means, but congratulations nonetheless."

"It means that a lot of new doors are opening."

"Wow. You're thinking about going out on your own?"

"It's a possibility. Something I've been thinking about for a while now."

"Looking for artistic freedom?"

"That's some of it. I must admit, though, after spending time with Imps and Cherubims, I've also been thinking about doing something to encourage more music education for local kids. Some kind of outreach or something. Not sure what, exactly, but the label and the studio can be part of that."

This was a new aspect of Connor, and Vivi's chest

warmed at the generosity of spirit it displayed. Connor was quick to write a check, but this would be something more than just distant philanthropy. Her mind immediately began to whirl, thinking of community programs, fundraising opportunities...

The habits of a lifetime in non-profit work, though, didn't stop another thought from barging in, and the whirl of ideas ground to a halt. "So this means you're moving home? Full-time?"

He shook his head. "Not full-time, but I'm going to convert the top floor into an apartment for me, because I do plan to be in town a lot more in the future."

Oh. She didn't know what to say to that. This fling with Connor was doable and reasonable and understandable because he was only here temporarily. Being reckless and bad could be acceptable if it were only for a short while. If she'd known he was planning on re-establishing a base here...

And they were about to be very publicly connected...

Damn it. Things had just gotten really complicated.

NINE

—

There was a reason LaSalle stayed booked. Sure, it was trendy, and the current hot spot created by a celebrity chef, but in Connor's experience, trendy hot spots were usually highly overrated. LaSalle, though... Another bite of the bread pudding might kill him, but letting it go to waste seemed like a cardinal sin.

Vivi eyeballed the last bite, but put her fork down and admitted defeat. "I simply can't. You're going to have to carry me out of here as it is."

"I was hoping you'd carry me."

"Then we'll just have to sit here until we can walk." She sipped at her coffee. "In my case, that's looking like sometime next week."

"Sitting is an excellent idea."

While the view across the table from him had kept the internal fires stoked, he was, unbelievably enough, having an excellent time anyway. Vivi's simple black dress clung to every curve, and the neckline was just low enough to showcase the gentle swell of her cleavage and classic double string of pearls without crossing over into a tacky advertisement of her charms. She'd pulled her hair up into some kind of fancy twist, leaving the elegant column of her neck bare.

He wanted her, but anticipation was part of the attraction and excitement. He wasn't in a rush—well, he *was,* but he was enjoying this, too.

After so long on the road, and living that life, he'd forgotten what it was like to be in the company of a *lady.* A well-bred, well-mannered, well-spoken, real Southern lady. Of course, he wouldn't expect Vivi to be anything less, but to his amazement he was utterly captivated by it. By *her.*

Vivi was sharp and smart; she had both the business sense and the non-profit experience to converse about his ideas for ConMan and outreach to the community. They had enough in common for conversation to flow easily, yet they were different enough to keep it interesting. She never bored him, and he was someone who was bored easily. She was gracious and amusing and charming, and she wasn't the least bit impressed by him. The honesty was refreshing. His ego should be smarting, but it made her responses genuine.

Now Connor understood why his father always cringed at his West Coast love affairs with starlets and musicians. In comparison to someone like Vivi... There simply wasn't a comparison.

Vivi's smile faded a little and she looked uncomfortable again as three people on the sidewalk pressed against the window of LaSalle, pointing and waving. One even tried to put a camera against the glass for a picture. Other patrons of the restaurant looked annoyed, but Vivi's discomfort got his attention.

"Just try to ignore it, Vivi."

"How? You can't even take a taxi or eat in peace. How do you ignore it?"

"It takes practice. Mainly I just try to remember that for some people celebrity-spotting is the biggest or best thing that's happened to them today. Or maybe even this week or this month. They'll post it to Facebook and Twitter and impress their friends and that will make them happy."

"At your expense?"

"Like I said, I owe my career to a million people I've never met. It seems a little petty to complain now."

She nodded, but picked up her coffee and turned slightly away from the window.

"Come on, Vivi, I know it's been a while, but surely you remember what it's like for people to want that brush with fame. You've done the photo ops."

"Yes, but not like this. People didn't normally recognize me unless I was wearing a crown and sash. Even then, they didn't know my name or who I was beyond Miss Louisiana. I wasn't famous. My *title* was famous. That's a big difference."

"That's not true."

"Fine. Name one Miss Louisiana other than me," she challenged.

She had him there. "Uh…"

"I'll go even easier. Who's the current Miss America? Or any Miss America *other* than Vanessa Williams."

Since he'd have been hard-pressed even to come up with Vanessa Williams, he had to admit defeat. "Regardless, you're still Vivienne LaBlanc. Everyone in New Orleans knows you."

"But they don't stalk me at restaurants to take my picture."

"Would you want them to?"

"You know, that kind of fame sounds good in theory, but now that I've seen it in practice..." She looked out the window, where the crowd had grown. "Maybe not."

"I can't control the paparazzi—not the professionals and not the amateurs. They come with the territory. If that's a problem for you..."

Vivi studied her napkin. He could almost see the wheels spinning inside her head. She finally looked up and met his eyes. "Lorelei says that we'll be on every blog by midnight."

"She's not wrong."

"I never planned on being infamous."

"You will be by morning."

He saw understanding dawn in her eyes. "I didn't think this through all the way. Did you?"

He didn't have to "think this through." This was just his life. "Vivi, you yourself said that tonight would make this public."

She swallowed. "I don't think I quite realized *how* public."

Time for those hard truths he'd promised her. "Until now your comings and goings at Gabe's have gone unnoticed. Once those pictures hit the blogs, there's a good chance someone will remember that they saw you there. Other people will start looking for you. If you walk out of here with me tonight there's no going back. You'll just have to ride it out."

"And if I don't?"

He took a deep breath. "No one could really blame me for trying to charm you. And we could claim that tonight's dinner had something to do with Saints and Sinners. There will still be speculation, but it'll fade. You have quite the reputation around here as a good girl, so folks will believe you. But, of course, that will be it for us."

Connor didn't like the rock that settled in his stomach as he said that. But Vivi had to realize that truth. And so did he. It had to be said, if for no other reason than to make *him* acknowledge it. The importance of this moment had sneaked up on him. He didn't like that.

"There's no way we can sneak around when everyone's looking out for just that."

Vivi blew out her breath in a long sigh. "Good Lord, I thought this was just going to be a quiet dinner. I had no idea it was some kind of point of no return."

Indeed. Vivi had a choice to make—and he had to, in all fairness, give her the opportunity to make it. Part of him wanted to argue his case, but he resisted. Instead, he signaled for the check, putting the ball in her court. "If you're going, now's a good time. Have the *maître d'* call you a cab and be seen by that crowd getting into it *alone.*"

"I understand." She fell quiet.

So did he, but he wasn't expecting the disappointment that had come with her words. Boy, this was a record even for him. He shouldn't care. They'd had their fun; they could part ways now, before ugliness set in to make the future unpleasant. But something unfamiliar spread through his stomach at the thought of Vivi walking out now. His cynical inner voice told him it would be better and safer if she did, but it didn't stop him from hoping that she might not. That hope left his inner cynic howling a protest that told *him* to get out now.

What a mess. And in public, too. He left a hefty tip— even bigger than usual—so if the server was asked about tonight she'd have a good story to tell and maybe keep from mentioning anything she'd inadvertently overheard. He pocketed the receipt, but Vivi still sat there.

"Well?"

She picked up her purse. "I'm ready when you are."

It took a minute for her words to sink in, but even as they did he kept his optimism on a short leash. The *maître d'* stepped outside to shoo the crowd away from the door and flagged down a taxi.

It coasted to a stop at the curb, and Vivi still seemed like she was going to go through with this. He wasn't holding his breath, though. Vivi had a lot on the line. When he stepped outside, the flashes seemed blinding after the tastefully dim interior of LaSalle. Vivi kept her eyes on the buttons of her coat at first, but then she stepped forward and tucked her hand under his arm.

He wasn't prepared for the effect that simple gesture would have on him.

A gasp rose from the gathered crowd. Or maybe that was just his brain misfiring in shock. Head held high,

Vivi looked calm, like she *hadn't* just tortured herself over this mere minutes ago. It was a small gesture, but one that would be as good as gold for the bloggers. People started shouting questions, but Vivi let him help her into the taxi, and then, in full view of the gawking crowd, kissed him as he closed the door behind them.

"You've done it now."

She smiled. "I know."

"Why, Vivi?"

"Because you only live once. And right now I'm not ready to be done with this."

A week ago, Vivi had convinced herself that Connor's predictions were overstated and hysterical. Now—well, she wanted to be angry at him for his knack for understatement. She felt like she was living in a damn circus.

She'd had an uptick in attention after the announcement of the Sinner and Saint, but it had mostly been local. The non-local attention had really just been reflected off Connor. It had been noticeable, but small. But now...

The email address for the gallery overflowed with interview requests, questions and fan mail she was supposed to pass along to Connor. She'd had to turn the ringer off on the phone at the gallery days ago, before the constant noise drove everyone insane, and now she just checked the voice mail a few times a day. Thankfully no one had gotten hold of her personal email address or her cell phone number, so she could still do some business. The gallery itself was hopping, but it was mostly gawkers, not buyers, and she'd had to hire additional staff just for crowd control. She certainly couldn't be in there during opening hours; she'd learned that just two days after their "quiet dinner" had exploded.

Her address had gotten out very easily, and plenty of people now stalked her house, either hoping for a glimpse of Connor or hoping to get a comment from her. Her house didn't have a fence or a gated courtyard, so people could just walk up to her front door—and many had. No wonder Connor had never come to her house. After she'd found one photographer hiding in the bushes under her bedroom window, Daddy had finally hired a private security firm to keep them off her property.

Lorelei had enjoyed the attention at first, but it had gotten old fast for her, too, and she was spending more time at their parents' house—which *did* have a nice big fence to keep people away.

Lord, just the walk from the gallery to Connor's apartment was like running a gauntlet sometimes. And with people from all over coming in for the parades and the Mardi Gras celebrations, there always seemed to be a fresh onslaught.

And, coming off Connor's recent run in the tabloids, everyone wanted to know who she was—who she used to be. If one more picture of her in crown and sash hit the papers she might barf. There were plenty of photos of her that were far more current, but everyone loved the beauty queen angle. The press was having a heyday with Bad-Boy Connor and Good-Girl Vivi from past to present. There was a quest for dirt on her, but at least she knew she was safe there: she really *was* a good girl and there was no dirt to be found.

But even her reputation didn't stop folks from speculating—pretty graphically, at times—about what she and Connor were up to. Every day she hated Katy Arras and her lies a little more.

They were certainly a popular couple, regardless of the speculation. At first, being dropped into Connor's world had been jarring. She hadn't realized how difficult it really was to be *that* famous. Everything Connor did—what he wore, where he went, what he ate—was interesting to someone, somewhere.

And that made her interesting to people as well.

She'd been offered several ways to cash in on her newfound notoriety and popularity and at Connor's insistence had hired a manager to field those offers. While many of the offers seemed like seedy and skeevy ways to cash in on her fame quickly, this circus had re-ignited a part of her career she'd thought long behind her. She was being asked to speak to groups—maybe even consider writing a book—on the platforms she'd promoted as Miss Louisiana, the work she'd done since then in non-profits and the arts, all the way up to and including beauty tips. It was like the whole country had woken up and decided she might have something worthwhile to say. Her fifteen minutes weren't quite up, it seemed, which was both good and bad.

What kind of world was it where fame came knocking solely because of who you dated? *Welcome to the era of the internet and twenty-four-hour news. It made people famous for sleeping with someone famous.*

Ugh. Her faith in humanity was being sorely tried.

The sad and slightly scary part, though, was that she really didn't mind. She was having *that* good of a time. Top of the list of Things She Thought She Would Never, Ever Say was *Connor is totally worth it*. Yet he was.

And that might be the truly freaky part. Connor had offered her an escape route, and she'd walked right by. She'd told herself at LaSalle that nothing had really changed beyond public awareness and a less definite timeframe, but that wasn't proving to be true. There was something *else*—something she wasn't quite willing to explore too deeply yet—that made the circus totally worthwhile.

All in all, this was the oddest experience of her life—dwarfing even the madness of the Miss America contest—but it was also the most incredible. So, in that way, it kind of balanced out.

Either that or she was totally losing her mind.

Vivi shut down her computer and turned off the lights in the gallery's office. She'd come in an hour ago at closing time to catch up on some paperwork, but focus wouldn't come. *At least I got the bills paid.* The electricity would stay on and the staff would get their paychecks, so that was enough for tonight.

Officially, Saints and Sinners only had six days left before the winner was announced and the fundraiser came to an end with the rest of the city's celebrations. Tomorrow would be their last public event until the winner took his or her place on top of the Bon Argent float on Tuesday morning. While the final five days— Friday to midnight Tuesday—would be the busiest for the city as a whole, they would be amazingly calm for her and Connor. Everyone had other plans—this was one of the busiest weekends of the entire year—so even as the flavor of the moment for the media, thanks to Connor, she was looking at a relatively low-key weekend.

But first she had a quiet evening at Connor's planned for tonight.

An anticipatory shiver ran through her and put speed in her steps as she gathered her stuff, set the alarm and locked the doors to the gallery behind her. A glance up showed two feet propped on the balcony railing. She couldn't see Connor from this vantage point, but he could probably see her, so she smiled before she stepped into the street. The feet disappeared, and by the time she'd made it to the nondescript wooden door, the sound of the buzzer releasing the lock was greeting her.

Connor met her at the top of the stairs with a kiss that had her toes curling in pleasure. "'Bout time you showed up."

Vivi dropped her bags and left her shoes by the door before following Connor into the kitchen. She took the glass of wine he offered with a grateful sigh and took a sip. "I spent some time on the phone with a reporter from the *LA Times*. He's doing a story on post-Katrina reconstruction."

"And he called *you*?"

"Gee, you don't have to sound so surprised."

Connor schooled his features. "Sorry, it's just that doesn't seem like your area of expertise."

"I know. But people think reconstruction is all about houses, and this was more about the effects on people.

Loss of community, effects on children and families, the over-stretched resources of non-profits…"

Connor nodded in understanding. "And that *is* your area of expertise."

"Exactly. My new manager has been out full force getting my name in front of people."

He refilled both of their glasses and leaned against the counter. "Raymond's awesome at finding those angles."

"Well, I appreciate the recommendation. I had no idea it would explode like this."

"And you didn't even have to release a sex tape."

She snorted. "Don't think for a second that I haven't been offered a hell of a lot of money for exactly that."

"Good thing you're a saint." He lifted his glass to hers in a toast.

She sighed and took a big sip of wine. "You know, you're suddenly being vindicated just because I *am* such a saint."

"Don't think I don't know it. It's much appreciated."

Nodding at his battered blue jeans and well-worn black and gold jersey, she untucked her blouse from her pants and started removing the heavy necklace and bracelet she'd worn that day. "So, you seem to have spent the day lounging on the balcony? Must be nice."

"Hey, I was working," he informed her. "I talked to an interior designer about plans for the warehouse, approved a licensing agreement for some music, went over the final figures from the tour with my accountant—"

"All from the comfort of your balcony?"

Connor grinned. "The job has to come with some perks, you know."

"I want to be a rock star. Think I'm too old to get my big break?"

He laughed. "Age isn't the problem, Vivi. The fact you're tone-deaf, though, is an obstacle."

She smacked his arm and frowned at him. He responded with a shrug and a grin. "I am *not* tone-deaf," she insisted.

"You are many wonderful things, Vivi, and you have many great talents, but I've heard you sing in the shower. You couldn't carry a tune in a bucket if I put the tune in the bucket and handed it to you."

He was right, but... "Wow, I may swoon from the flattery."

Connor snorted. "Because I'm the one you can always come to for empty flattery?"

"Point taken."

That was why this worked. Connor was, oddly enough, the one person she could drop any and all attempts at pretense with. It wasn't as if he could think worse of her than he had at some point in the past. It was a very strange situation—and an unusual way to find that acceptance of who she really was—but it worked for her. It made it easy.

He took the wineglass from her hand and set it behind her on the counter. Then he lifted her up, sat her on the counter, and moved between her legs. "You've had a long day. Are you hungry? Tired?"

One minute ago she'd have said yes, but Connor asked the questions with his lips against her neck, and the need for food or rest gave way to a much more simple, primal need.

His mouth found hers, and she sighed into him with a release she'd never felt with anyone before. It should be scary, but it wasn't.

It felt pretty close to perfect.

TEN

—

"It's six o'clock in the morning," Lorelei grumped as she pushed past Vivi to the coffeepot. "Could you stop the humming? Your constant good mood is making me ill."

"Aren't you a ray of sunshine this morning?"

Lorelei held the cup of coffee like a lifeline. "Do you not need sleep like normal humans?"

"I'm just in a good mood this morning."

"As usual."

"What?"

"I feel like I'm living in a Disney movie. I'm expecting you to burst into song while woodland creatures clean the house and make you a dress for the ball."

"Well, that would be interesting, wouldn't it? I'm rather tone-deaf, and I'm not sure that gators and nutria have the same dexterity and sewing skills as bunnies and chipmunks." Vivi winked at her sister, but refrained from more humming as she left the kitchen.

Lorelei followed. "See—I can't even get a rise out of

you by making fun of you. Where's the sanctimonious Vivi I know and love?"

"Poor Lorelei. You're living a nightmare."

Lorelei made a face as she took her usual spot in the corner of the couch. "I'm glad you're happy, but do you *have* to be so chipper about it?"

"Boy, you're grumpy. Drink your coffee. I like you better when you're fully caffeinated." She patted Lorelei on the arm. "I've got to go. I'm going straight to Connor's after we're done today, so I'll see you in the morning."

"Surprise, surprise," Lorelei muttered.

"Something wrong?"

"No." Lorelei took another sip of coffee. "Actually, yes. Something is wrong."

"Okay, what?"

"You." Lorelei's stare was unsettling. "You're not quite right these days."

"Excuse me?"

"This is really not like you."

"I know. It's crazy. But it's fun. And you wanted me to have fun, right?"

"Of course. But how deep are you into this thing with Connor?"

That brought her up short. "What do you mean?"

"You have never, not once in your life, had a fling, an affair, or a one-night stand. You are a serial monogamist at best. Now you're sleeping—very publicly, I might add—with Connor. You spend all of your free time—and even time that's not free—with him. From where I stand, it looks like you're getting serious about this."

"Then why do you sound like the Oracle of Doom?"

"Because Connor isn't really a smart long-term investment. I don't want you to get hurt." Lorelei put her coffee cup on the table and leveled a hard stare at her. "Are you in love with Connor?"

The concept had been floating around in her mind, but it wasn't something she was willing to explore too deeply. "What?"

"It's a very simple question. Are you in love with Connor?"

She tried to be nonchalant. "You're jumping ahead a bit, aren't you? This is still very new."

"Well, are you and Connor on the same page at least?"

"Are you asking me if we've had a 'Where is this going?' conversation?" The mere idea of such a thing seemed totally out of the question. "No. We haven't."

Lorelei looked at her like she'd lost her mind. "And that doesn't bother you? Have aliens taken over your body?"

It did bother her a little. But Connor wasn't the kind of man she'd be comfortable having that kind of conversation with. "No. It just seems a bit premature to be talking about it."

Vivi could almost hear Lorelei's eyeballs rolling. "You've never walked blindly into anything in your life. You always have a plan. A purpose. You have to have some kind of plan cooking in there."

Why did Vivi feel like the younger sister? "My plan is to see how it goes. There's definitely something. I don't think it's love. It could be hormones or infatuation or any number of things. It's a very strong *like*, though, and I'm willing to explore that and enjoy it now, for what it is. There's no need for me to rush into this." She met Lorelei's eyes. "I'm an adult. I can handle this—whatever it is, whatever it becomes. Or doesn't become."

"Vivi—"

"Look, I've got to get ready to go. But I promise you that it's all good. I'm fine."

Lorelei didn't look convinced, but other than some deep sighs, she dropped the subject.

But Vivi was having a hard time doing the same. She couldn't keep skittering around the edges of this. At some point she was going to have to really decide. But not yet. She wanted to enjoy this as long as she could.

The street was quiet as Vivi locked the door behind her. She started down the stone steps, only to stop short when she saw Connor leaning against his rented red sportscar parked at the curb. He opened the passenger-side door as she approached.

"This is a surprise," she said.

"I'm full of surprises," he said as he helped her in. Once he was in his seat, he handed her a small bag. "Here."

"What's this?"

"Just something I happened to find yesterday at the French Market. Open it."

She did, allowing the contents to slide into her palm. It was a bracelet, and when she held it up she saw the charm: a halo hanging off a set of devil horns.

Connor winked at her. "I thought it might be appropriate."

"It's perfect." She leaned over the console and gave him a kiss. "Thank you."

"You're welcome." Connor started the engine.

Vivi dangled the bracelet from her fingers, admiring the charm. It wasn't an expensive gift; she could tell by looking at it that it wasn't the highest quality and might possibly turn her wrist green. But that was part of its charm. It wasn't a gift meant to impress— not beyond the thought behind it, at least. And that thought caused her chest to feel a bit tight.

She had to face it: she *was* in love with Connor. While it felt good to put a name to it, to admit to it, the happy feeling was short-lived due to reality. She'd fallen in love with a man who hadn't given her even the slightest of hints about his own feelings or what might lie ahead.

The enormous folly of that slammed into her like a bag of bricks, and no matter how hard she tried, she couldn't quite shake that feeling off to focus on the day's project.

The last day of the competition part of Saints and Sinners had them at a community center in one of the poorest areas of town. The teams were painting walls, washing windows and mulching the playground as part of a larger rehabilitation project. They were halfway through the day when Vivi realized she'd forgotten they were in competition at all. For the first time in, well...*ever,* her competitive streak had remained underground. She'd been too lost in the mess inside her own head even to compete properly.

It took a real effort of will—and garnered her some strange looks from both sides—to pull Team Saint back together so they'd take the points. Only once they were safely in her column did she go back to help Connor paint the hallway.

"Hate to say it, but you lose. Again."

He winked at her. "I wondered when you'd remember."

"I can't believe you took advantage of me like that."

Connor shook his head. "I don't look gift horses in the mouth and I don't question my luck. I need you in order to get through this without looking like a loser in front of the press."

Something about the words—or maybe the tone—put her hackles up. "Is that all you want from me?"

"Given a choice, I'd rather not be here at all. We'd be at Gabe's on a rug in front of the fireplace drinking mimosas. Trust me, Vivi. What I want from you right now doesn't involve painting a wall. And it certainly doesn't include two dozen bystanders."

Well, gee, if she'd been looking for a declaration of some sort, that certainly wasn't it.

"All I ask from you is honesty. If you want something, just ask. Don't try to charm it out of me."

That got her an odd look from Connor. "What are you talking about?"

Her spurt of bravado fled the scene. She was not going to be the one to broach that topic, and she certainly wasn't going to do it *here*, of all places. She had her pride. "Nothing." She forced a smile. "You may be able to addle my mind with orgasms, but you will not be able to woo me to the dark side with your charms. I'm made of sterner stuff than that."

She waited for Connor to wink or shrug or crack

off a smart comeback, but none of those things happened. Instead, Connor's paintbrush hit the bucket with a splat, and she found herself being led—almost dragged, actually—into an empty activity room, where he closed the door behind him.

Déjà vu. "That door better not lock from the outside. After our recent publicity, no one will believe we *weren't* up to something in here." It was a lame attempt at a joke and it fell flat.

Connor crossed his arms over his chest. "Explain."

"I don't know what you mean."

"I've known you a hell of a long time, Vivi, and that was a loaded statement. I'd like to know what you meant by it."

Damn. "I think you're reading a bit much into a few words."

"Again, I know you better than that."

The calm assurance caused her temper to flare. "Actually, Connor, I don't think you know me at all. Which isn't entirely surprising, since I'm beginning to think that I don't know myself very well either. My whole life has flipped upside down."

Connor had the gall to look surprised. "So has mine, you know."

"Really? I figured this was par for the course for you."

"No." He shook his head. "*This* is definitely new territory."

"I don't think we're talking about the same thing."

There was that odd look again. "What are *you* talking about, Vivi?"

"I asked you first."

"Vivi..."

"Fine." This was neither the time nor the place, but she'd led the way here and there wasn't a graceful way to turn back now. "We have five days left of Saints and Sinners. What happens *six* days from now?"

"I don't know about you, but I'll be sleeping in."

His attempt to dodge her question only highlighted the necessity of asking it. She *needed* those answers she'd blithely dismissed this morning. "Okay, ten days from now? Two weeks? A month?"

Connor looked like he'd swallowed something vile. *Well, there's my answer.* Better to get it now. "That's what I thought."

He shoved his hands into his jeans pockets. "Are you looking for some kind of declaration of intent? I hadn't really thought that far in advance."

"I have to, sadly. It feels like the whole country is watching me, so I need to prepare for the aftermath. This whole thing with you has been a departure from the norm, and I need to be ready to deal with the fall-out."

"You're jumping way ahead—"

"Actually, I'm trying to fall back. I jumped ahead of myself getting involved with you so quickly. Now I'm just regrouping and preparing for what comes next."

"And what do you think that is?"

"I really don't know. So much is happening so quickly—"

He stepped closer to her and reached for her arms. "So why not wait until things calm down before we have this conversation? Can't we just continue on as we are and see where it goes?"

"If you were anyone other than Connor Mansfield I'd say yes." She pulled her arms out of his hands gently. This hurt more than she'd expected, which only strengthened her resolve that it was the right thing to do. Now, before she got any more attached and Connor did serious damage to her heart. "I stand to lose a lot more than you do if this ends badly. Maybe we should quit while we're ahead."

Connor couldn't quite believe his ears. How had they gotten here? Talk about things coming from left field... "What are you saying, Vivi?"

"I'm saying that I can't invest in something that doesn't have a future. I thought I could. I thought I could just seize the day and not worry. But I'm not a fling kind of girl, and you're not a long-haul kind of guy."

She might as well have slapped him. He felt unfairly vilified. "So you dipped your toes in the pool, decided it was too hot and are now pulling out?"

"No. I jumped completely in. But now I think the pool is too dangerous for me to swim in. You know me well enough, Connor, to know that I'm a good girl. I'm not cut out to be flavor of the month."

Vivi seemed genuinely distressed at the idea. Distressed enough to make him want to play Lancelot and soothe her. "I had no intention of getting involved with anyone when I came home. After the disaster of the last few months the last thing I wanted was to have my love life back in the papers at all. Much less with you. No offense intended."

Vivi actually cracked a smile. "None taken."

He hooked a finger through her belt loop and pulled her an inch closer to him. She didn't resist. He used a finger to lift her chin, making her look him straight in the eye. "I didn't expect this, didn't plan on it and if anyone had tried to tell me it was going to happen I'd have laughed in their face. At the same time, though, I'm not unhappy it did."

"Oh, me neither. It's been fun."

"It *is* fun. And it can continue to be fun. I know it's tough for you to deal with the carnival sideshow that is my life, but believe me when I say it gets easier. You can't live worrying about how your life is being interpreted or judged by the wider world. That way lies only madness." He saw Vivi's eyebrows draw together. "And remember you have a manager now. Damage control is his job, because his paycheck rather depends on you. Is he telling you to dump me?"

She shook her head. "I think you're missing my point."

Oh, he hadn't missed it; he'd just hoped he could sidestep it. No such luck. He wasn't going to get off that easily. He took a deep breath, rather wishing he'd let that statement in the hallway slide. "When it comes to women, I'm not used to thinking too far ahead. The only thing I can say is that I'm not ready for this to be over yet. Are you? Really?"

"Honestly?" She seemed to think about it. "No."

He let out the breath he'd been holding. "I don't have a lot of experience with women like you, but I'm not willing to give it up just yet." This was an odd place and time for him to be having this kind of revelatory discussion, but the weight in his chest wouldn't allow him to just let Vivi walk out.

Those blue eyes were wide and luminous. "So we let it play out?"

"Yeah. Can you do that? Just wait and see what happens?"

There was that silence again that had him holding his breath. He felt a bit foolish.

Finally Vivi nodded. "I think so. I'll try, at least."

"That's all I ask, Vivi." In reality, he knew he was asking a lot from her, and he was beyond relieved to see her nod. He leaned down to give her a kiss, only to have her jump back when someone knocked on the door.

Vivi's smile twisted. "They're looking for us."

"Of course they are. Come on." He tucked her hand in his and opened the door.

Vivi wasn't the only one in uncharted waters. This was completely new for him, too. Usually, though, he liked uncharted waters. They were exciting. They kept life interesting. He'd just never gone off without a map in his personal life before.

He reminded himself that he hadn't made it this far without taking chances. Vivi seemed to be a chance he was willing to take. One that might be worth taking.

And that was a new feeling.

Although few would believe it, Connor hadn't been home for a single parade in years. There just hadn't been time. Even fewer would believe that after such a hiatus Connor Mansfield wouldn't be part of the throngs of people on the streets partying—after all, that was part of the brand he'd built.

No one would believe, though, that he'd spend Saturday—the first major day of revelry—at a family friend's house on St. Charles Street, eating burgers off the grill and watching the parades from a balcony set back from the road and separated from the people by a large fence. It wasn't quiet by any stretch of the imagination—not between the crowds and the thirty or so people gathered in the Devereauxes' home—but the fence separated the public bacchanal from the family party nicely.

Angie, fresh off an afternoon on Bourbon Street, looked a little worse for wear when she returned around sunset. Angie was in her forties, her dark blond hair showing small streaks of gray like highlights. Seeing his all-business, L.A.-glam agent in jeans, with her usually perfectly coiffed hair askew and piles of colorful beads ringing her neck, was almost amusing.

"Wow! I kinda love this town," she said.

"It does have its charms."

"But to leave the French Quarter—which was almost scary at times—to come here..." She looked pointedly at the group of kids playing in the yard and the tables full of food. "It's a bit of a disconnect."

"This is how I remember most Mardi Gras growing up. I did the crazier stuff in high school, but as a kid... Well, all kids love a parade, right?"

"Not quite Norman Rockwell, but still very family-friendly. I wouldn't have believed it."

He smiled as he offered her another beer. "You

might as well get comfortable and grab something to eat. We have a little time before the parade arrives."

"And you'll be on one of those floats on Tuesday, right?"

"Yep. The Sinner and the Saint and the whole court. Bon Argent doesn't run its own parade, but since it's a charity krewe, another krewe is more than willing to let us parade with them every year."

Surprise crossed Angie's face. "*Us?* You've joined up or something?"

"Of course. Membership for the Saint and Sinner is honorary, if they're not already members, but they've asked me to serve on the board next year."

"And you're going to do it?"

Why was Angie looking at him like that? "Of course. Why wouldn't I?"

"As your agent, I should probably know about these things before they're a done deal."

"It's a volunteer position. I don't get paid for it, so it doesn't really require your input."

"It's not the money, Connor. Your plate is quite full at the moment—"

"And you would know, since you're the one filling it," he interrupted.

She smiled like that was a compliment. "You seem to be trying to rearrange everything to center around New Orleans."

"Everyone needs a home base. I've decided to make my home my home base."

Angie sighed and shook her head. "This is Vivi's influence on you, isn't it?"

"What?"

"I feel like I'm staging an intervention." Setting down her beer, Angie clasped her hands in her lap and leaned forward. "I like Vivi. She's a nice girl, and a role model for many, but she's not *your* role model." She looked over to where Vivi, Lorelei and Jennie Devereaux were loading yet more food—and a King Cake—onto an already groaning table. "I know you're enjoying this, but don't screw up everything we've worked so hard for over the years."

We've. Like it had been a real joint effort. "I'm not screwing anything up. I'm just enjoying the benefits."

"Good." Angie nodded like a bobble-head doll. "Do that. Everyone should. Vivi certainly is, but you have a lot more to lose."

He was not in the mood for this. "Angie, if there's something you want to say, just say it. Quit beating around the bush."

"All right, then. I find it very interesting that out of nowhere you hook up with some local girl—"

"It's not out of nowhere," he corrected. "I've known Vivi my whole life."

Angie rolled her eyes. "Oh, it sounds all romantic, but when did you start believing your own lyrics? Step back for a minute. You yourself told me how this girl has hated you most of your life, yet she suddenly gets over it now that you're famous? That sounds a bit opportunistic to me."

"You're cynical, Ange."

"No, I'm realistic. Three weeks ago she was an aging beauty queen-slash-socialite with a small gallery in New Orleans. This week she's on the cover of

People. You know exactly the type of woman I'm talking about."

"I do. But you don't know Vivi. That's not her style at all."

"Really? And you know this *how*? Connor, her face is everywhere right now. She's had to hire a manager, companies are pitching reality TV shows to her, and she's suddenly a commodity on the speaker circuit... She went from nobody to somebody in record time, and all she had to do was sleep with you."

An unusual feeling, someplace between dread and anger, settled on his chest. Who or what it was directed at was a mystery. "There's a causal relationship, sure. But that doesn't imply forethought."

"But it should give *you* second thoughts, at least. Especially now that you're toying with ideas that could put your career back *years*."

It shouldn't give him second thoughts, but Angie's earnestness forced him to consider it. He pushed it away as quickly as he could. "You're making all kinds of connections where there aren't any, and assigning motives where none exist. That smacks of paranoia."

"You're not my first or only client. After some of the crap I've seen, I sound like Pollyanna right now. I only want what's best for you, Connor."

Others might think Angie was mothering him with her concern, but Connor knew Angie didn't have a maternal bone in her body. She didn't even like live houseplants. They weren't friends. This was business.

"Or do you want what makes you the most money?"

"Honey, that's one and the same. Your success is

my paycheck, but it's still your success and your paycheck. Let's not make any rash decisions you'll regret."

Right now his only regret was allowing his agent to attend a social event. Angie had soured his good mood. Her assertions were far-fetched at best, but he was too much of a cynic—or maybe he had had a little too much of spotlight-seeking women recently—to dismiss them completely out of hand.

But this was *Vivi* Angie was talking about...

The crowd on the street roared to life, and Vivi appeared a second later to put a hand on his shoulder. "That's the parade. You two coming?"

Connor had learned early on that no one in this business really cared about him—beyond what he could do for them, at least. Angie was just protecting her turf and the biggest cash cow in the herd. She had no life outside business and didn't understand anyone who did.

He stood and let Vivi catch his hand. *No.* This thing with Vivi was the realest thing that had happened to him in a long time.

Glancing over at Angie, he smiled. "I don't believe in regrets."

ELEVEN

—

Rain came in Monday night, making Vivi worry, but Tuesday morning dawned clear. Vivi watched the morning weather report, cup of coffee in hand, and smiled when the meteorologist promised a sunny and mild afternoon. She'd both sweated and shivered through Mardi Gras in the past, but today might not be a bad day to spend in satin and angel wings.

"You're up early," Connor mumbled as he passed her on his way to the kitchen for coffee, pausing only to drop a kiss on the top of her head.

"It's a big day."

It certainly felt momentous already. Although it had been hard at times, Vivi had never spent the whole night with Connor, choosing instead to make her way home in the wee hours of the night. There'd been a couple of mornings where she'd barely made it home before dawn—which might be splitting hairs—but yesterday afternoon she'd purposefully packed a bag with the intent of staying all night. Waking up to sunshine peeking around the curtains and Connor snuggled firmly behind her had certainly felt momentous.

Connor came back with a steaming mug and read the weather ticker off the bottom of the screen. He looked sleep-rumpled and freshly rolled-out-of-bed-sexy, whereas she'd taken a couple of minutes to wash her face and brush her hair. He looked delicious, no matter what, but she didn't have quite the same confidence.

"You okay?" he asked.

She didn't have to ask about what. Connor's call had come from Max about nine o'clock last night, congratulating him on his win. Although she'd been next to Connor on the couch, and heard Connor's side of the entire conversation, she'd waited for Max to call her a few minutes later to break the news to her. They'd been a little preoccupied with other activities, though, and hadn't had much of a chance to discuss it.

"Of course. I'm disappointed, but I reconciled myself to this weeks ago. All things considered, I think I put in a good showing, and we raised a ton of money."

"That's Pageant Vivi talking."

"I've had practice at being a gracious loser."

"You can still ride up top with me, you know."

"I will not flout tradition like that. *You* will be on top, where you belong."

"But I like it when you're on top."

That statement had Vivi trying to calculate how much time they had this morning before they had to leave for the parade. Traffic would be terrible, but...

They were half an hour late. But everyone and everything seemed to be running late as well, so they spent another twenty minutes hanging around. Well, *she* hung around; Connor signed autographs and smiled for cameras with fans from their host krewe and riders on the floats. She rather wished she'd brought a book.

"Congratulations, Vivi."

Angie stood behind her, slightly overdressed for the event, with big black sunglasses covering her eyes. Vivi knew that Angie was very good at her job, but Vivi didn't like her all that much. There was something about her that was just off-putting. She was just too brusque and focused on the bottom line for Vivi's taste.

"I will say thanks, because it's over and we did a great job, but they haven't officially announced anything. All congratulations are technically premature."

"I'd say you did pretty well, regardless."

"Thank you. I was afraid Connor would simply stomp me, but I think I held my own."

"I didn't mean in the competition—but kudos to you, of course, for that."

She couldn't see Angie's eyes for the sunglasses, but the slightly mocking smile put her on alert. "Then I'm afraid I don't know what you mean."

"It doesn't really matter if you win or lose this competition. I'd think you'd be proud of yourself either way."

What was Angie getting at? "I am. Like I said, Saints and Sinners has been a great success."

"You're certainly reaping the benefits."

Okay, there was definitely a snort in there. Vivi lost patience. "Angie, if there's something you want to say, please just say it. I'm really not in the mood for games."

"You've managed to ride this little event straight into the spotlight...on Connor," she finished crudely.

"Excuse me?"

"Oh, you're quite clever, and I repeat my kudos. You certainly know how to take advantage of a situation. Nice write-up in the *Times,* by the way."

The insult and implication were obvious. Vivi felt her jaw gape in shock. "I won't deny that my relationship with Connor has opened up all kinds of new doors for me, but I'm not seeing Connor for that reason."

"Oh, honey, I'm not judging you—"

It sure sounds like it.

"I know all about how this game is played."

"This isn't a game. If you're worried about Connor—"

"I never worry about Connor. He's a pro. He knows how it works. This business creates strange bedfellows, but it's all still business in the end. A little *quid pro quo* is just part of it."

"Well, if there was supposed to be some *quid pro quo* Connor got the short end of that stick." Vivi tried to laugh it off, because outrage and insult were growing. Soon she'd be saying something she'd really regret.

"I don't worry about Connor. Saints and Sinners gave him a chance to do something to counterbalance the whole Katy Arras thing. I tried to tell him it would die down and pass in its own time, but he's not the patient type. He likes to be proactive, you know. Change the PR conversation himself."

Vivi felt a small rock settle in her stomach. So much for pure altruism. But what had she expected, really? Connor had had an opportunity to change the narrative surrounding him and he had. And he'd done a great job as the Sinner—raised the profile of the event... The fact that he'd benefitted personally and professionally didn't negate the entire experience.

Even if it did cheapen it a bit.

Vivi pulled herself back. It was a multilayered situation. It couldn't be pulled apart and overanalyzed. Even if she was tempted to do just that.

Angie shrugged and surveyed the crowds of people milling around. Vivi knew the body language and braced herself.

"Connor's a very smart guy. Hooking up with you was a brilliant idea."

That *definitely* wasn't a compliment. Vivi gathered up as much dignity as she could while wearing five-foot wings. "I like to think that Connor has very good taste." *Damn. That came out stiffer than she'd hoped.*

Angie looked her up and down. "Oh, certainly. He needed to find himself a good girl to vindicate him. It would have been better if he'd been able to go the whole redemption route—much more press that way, and people just eat it up—but your approval was almost as good as papal forgiveness. And brilliantly played by both of you. It was like a fairy tale or something. By the time he gets back home—L.A. home, that is—everyone will be claiming they never believed that woman to begin with."

"Connor has plans here, too."

Angie's eyebrows arched over her sunglasses again, and Vivi felt the look of amused pity even if she couldn't fully see it.

"Connor's full of ideas. Half of them never work out.

That's why he needs me. He always claims he's moving home after a tour, but once he's caught up on his sleep he forgets all about it." Angie shook her head. "I know Connor. I've known him since he was opening for second-string acts at crappy clubs. Whatever those plans are, I promise you that he will lose all interest very soon. He'll need to be back in the studio and back on the road."

The rock in Vivi's stomach grew and made her nauseous. She recognized the cattiness for what it was, but that didn't help allay the sick feeling. If this had come from anyone other than Angie, Vivi would easily have dismissed it as jealousy. But this had been delivered with unemotional, professional distance. Angie had no personal reason to unsheath her claws.

It was ridiculous, but that very ridiculousness gave it weight. And that weight settled into Vivi's stomach. Angie's phone rang. She answered it without so much as an *excuse me,* but Vivi was happy for the reprieve.

But she couldn't shake the sick feeling. It niggled at her, playing on insecurities she hadn't known she still had. By the time Max got everyone's attention for the official announcement, she felt green around the gills.

Vivi made her way to the float, where Connor met her at the makeshift stairs. It was similar to their pageantry on the night of the ball. They climbed slowly to the top and took their places behind the velvet pillow holding the Saint's halo and the Sinner's horns.

Max started his speech—a rundown of how much they'd accomplished with their various community projects and the amount of money raised. Even through her unease, Vivi felt a moment of pride at the amount. A huge cheer went through the crowd and Vivi tried to enjoy it.

"Team Sinner!"

There was another roar of approval, and Vivi shot an apologetic look at her team of Cherubim. Connor noticed and leaned down.

"Don't worry about them. Both courts get excellent seats at my next concert, but the losing team gets backstage passes as well."

The forethought and kindness of the gesture lightened the rock. Connor wasn't in this for just selfish reasons.

Max signaled her, and Vivi picked up her halo and presented it to Connor, who hoisted it above the float like a pirate flag. He then placed his horns back on his head. Vivi curtseyed, and Connor climbed to the top tier of the float, his Imps right behind him, and took his place on the enormous throne with the Saints and Sinners crest above him. She and her Cherubim would man the lower tier.

The float began to inch forward. She looked up at Connor's throne and found him staring at her. Once he'd caught her eye, he gave her a wink and a small wave. Then, a huge grin on his face, he leaned back, propped his feet on the railing, and stacked his hands behind his head. He seemed to be genuinely enjoying the moment.

Whatever Angie's problem was, Vivi wasn't going to convict Connor of anything on hearsay alone. And if Angie was wrong on one front, she was probably wrong on the other, too.

The drumline of the marching band began their

beat, and they were officially under way. The sun came out from behind a cloud, and the excitement of the kids around her was palpable.

Today was a day to celebrate—even if she was celebrating a loss. And for now she had beads to throw.

Connor dropped his and Vivi's wings by the door with a mental sigh of relief. Cool-looking or not, twelve hours in them was more than enough for any man. The chafing...

As if she'd read his mind, Vivi chuckled as she kicked off her shoes and dug a pair of sweatpants out of her overnight bag. "I told you to wear something underneath the harness. I learned my lesson after the last time."

Connor carried the three-foot Saints and Sinners trophy they'd presented to him at the end of the parade to the coffee table and set it down. "Think it's big enough?"

"No need to brag about it," Vivi grumbled.

He shook his head at her. "You are a poor loser."

"I am not. I just like trophies."

He shot her a disbelieving look.

"It's true. I do like trophies. Because you get them when you win."

"And you like to win," he added.

"I am a serious competitor," she corrected.

"And a poor loser."

Vivi shook her head at him. "Whatever. I will not lie and say I didn't want that trophy. Unhook me, please?"

She turned her back to him as she asked and looked out the French doors at the street below. The crowds in the French Quarter had reached their peak tonight, and even through the thick window glass he could hear the noise of the party a block over on Bourbon. Even Royal Street—with its lack of bars—was busy. If he could muster the energy, he *might* go out on the balcony and toss some beads to folks in the street, but right now even that seemed beyond his capability. In two hours, at midnight, the police would begin to clear the streets and Mardi Gras would be over.

The hooks of Vivi's dress opened under his fingers, but unlike the last time he'd done this, he found the soft cotton of an undershirt instead of soft skin. She was probably still sore from the harness, and it would have solved the chafing problem nicely. "You're lucky your dress covers you enough to wear something under the harness. How could I possibly wear a shirt under this getup?"

Vivi pulled her arms out of the dress and let it drop to the floor. Clad in only the undershirt and a tiny pair of lacy panties, she stretched and groaned in relief. It was a lovely, erotic view he was almost too tired to fully appreciate, but he was still disappointed when Vivi's legs disappeared into the purple sweats. Then she dropped to the couch and let her head rest against the arm.

"I'll call Ms. Rene in the morning and offer some advice for the next time she wants to put someone in wings. But not right now. I'm just too exhausted to move anymore. I just want a glass of wine, a seat that doesn't move under me and a little quiet."

Connor peeled the leather vest off and started unwinding the leather straps from around his arms.

"Amen to that. I was almost afraid you'd want to head out for the last couple of hours."

"No way. It was a fun day but, mercy, it's been a long one." She sighed. "I don't want to see or talk to another human being for several days."

"Including me?"

"You may stay—but only if you bring the wine over here," she conceded. "I'm not moving from this spot until tomorrow. Call me a party pooper if you wish, but stick a fork in me 'cause I'm done."

He grabbed the wine and two glasses and set them on the table next to Vivi. The leather pants were off next, and he felt much better immediately. Tossing them into the pile with Vivi's dress, he went to the bedroom and grabbed a pair of jeans.

As he returned, Vivi shot him a sly look. "However, please don't let me stop you from enjoying yourself out there."

"I may not leave this apartment for at least a week." He joined her on the couch, lifting her feet out of the way to sit before placing them in his lap. "But if anyone asks, it was your idea to stay in for the rest of the night. Connor Mansfield should be out there partying hard, not safe on his couch and contemplating sleep at ten o'clock."

She frowned at him, a little crinkle forming between her eyes. "That makes me sound like a drag on your social life."

He poured, and handed a glass to Vivi. "One of the greatest things about dating a saint, I've discovered, is that everyone expects you to rein me in, reform my wicked ways and get me accepted back into polite society."

Vivi stiffened, and the wineglass paused halfway to her mouth. "Really? Is that what I'm doing?"

The clipped words came from left field. "Huh?"

"I'm reforming you?" She removed her legs from his lap and pushed up to a seated position. "Bringing you back into the 'right' social circles because you're a good boy now?"

"You don't actually have to do anything, you know. It's the appearance that counts."

"I see." She swung her feet to the floor and put her glass back on the table. "Are you saying that getting involved with me was part of some larger PR stunt?"

For someone claiming exhaustion a few minutes ago, she certainly seemed to have energy to spare now. "What? No."

"But you do admit that being with me has cleaned up your image some?"

What did it matter? "Yes, but I'd already decided to try to make peace with you before we became anything at all."

"Why?"

"We've been through this, Vivi."

"No, I think we skipped this. When, *exactly*, did you decide you wanted a cease-fire?"

He thought. "I don't know. That first weekend, maybe? Why?"

"Actually, that's my next question for you."

"Why would I try to get past the ridiculous antagonism of our youth?" To his surprise, she nodded. "Because we're adults."

Vivi scrubbed a hand across her face. "And what brought you home this time, after so many years?"

Okay, new topic. He was too tired to keep up. "I was asked to do Saints and Sinners. Same as you. Vivi, what are you talking about?"

"I just want to know why you agreed to be the Sinner. For someone fresh off a paternity and sex scandal, proclaiming yourself a sinner seems a bit counterintuitive PR-wise."

"What better way to get past it all? It showed I had a good sense of humor and—"

"Made you look good, too?"

"Yes. Is that a problem, Vivi?"

"It kinda is, yeah."

"Why?"

"Because that's not what this is supposed to be about."

"I'm sorry that my motives aren't as pure as you'd like them to be, but that doesn't make them evil either. Bon Argent wanted to make money and increase their profile. Mission accomplished. Big round of applause. Everybody wins, right?"

Vivi was biting her bottom lip so hard the skin was turning white. She'd be drawing blood soon. "So was I...was *this*...part of your not entirely evil plan, too?"

"You're not making sense, Vivi."

"Actually, it's making perfect sense now. I can't believe I didn't see it before. Saint Vivienne was just the icing on your redemption cake. After all, if sweet Saint Vivi is on your side, you must be just a misunderstood and unfairly vilified sinner. It's so obvious now. I can't believe I fell for that 'bygones' and 'let's be adults' crap, much less slept with you. Lord, I am *such* a fool."

"Have you lost your mind? Where is all this coming from?"

"You used me."

"I didn't use you."

Vivi rolled her eyes. "It's Marie Lester all over again."

"Really? We're going back *there*?"

"You haven't changed at all."

"Only you seem to see it that way. I just wanted the war to end. I want to live in this town in peace, and I can't do that when we're always sniping at each other. I get enough hassle elsewhere, thanks. I never claimed otherwise."

"And sleeping with me?"

"I thought that was a mutual attraction. I didn't know I'd have to prove my intentions after the fact."

Vivi's eyes narrowed. That wary, distrustful and disapproving look he knew so well was back. It cut him to the quick and angered him at the same time.

"You don't believe me. Wow. That's just..." Even after everything, Vivi so easily thought the worst of him. Shaking his head, he walked over to Gabe's bar in search of something stronger than wine. "Have you been stewing on this the whole time, Vivi?"

"No."

The relief that rushed in at her denial was short-lived.

"Maybe at first, but I got swept up in you and everything else and didn't bother to think about anything. You know, I could've handled just being a fling. But a pawn in your overall career plan? That's just wrong. Maybe I might have been willing to play along if you'd just been honest with me from the start. It didn't have to be like this."

Her words hit him like a slap. "Until right now, I thought 'this' was pretty damn good."

She didn't say anything.

"Oh, get off your high horse, Vivi. *You* showed up at *my* door in the middle of the night. And *you're* the one who keeps coming back."

If looks could kill, he'd be dead on the floor in a puddle of blood right now.

"You don't see me hurling accusations about your motives simply because it worked out so well for *you.*"

Her jaw dropped. *"What?"*

"I'm not the only one who's benefitted from this. Being Connor Mansfield's flavor of the month seems to be much more beneficial than first runner-up in Miss America. Just when you thought your glory days were behind you..."

"Shut up! You know, I kinda felt bad about all that attention, but now...not so much. It's only fair that I get something out of this, too."

"Wow, it seems *I* should be the one fluttering about my wounded virtue and being used, not you."

"You have no one to blame but yourself, then. I was willing to just hope for civility during Saints and Sinners. You, though, started spouting all that garbage about the inherent foibles of teenage boys and asking for forgiveness—"

"Forgiveness? Honestly, sanctimonious doesn't even *begin* to describe your attitude. Your superiority com-

plex is unbelievable. Either you're fooling yourself, or you're working hard to fool everybody else, because you're nothing but a fraud."

Vivi was one of those rare women for whom anger was a good look. Pieces of her hair had come down from its ponytail, curling perfectly around the curve of her cheeks—which were flushed pink and brought out the blue in her eyes. Anger snapped in the air around them, and her chest heaved with it. But her eyes were clear—no false tears there.

Those eyes raked over him in cold disdain before her lip curled into a snarl. "Screw you, Connor."

Lips pressed together like she was dying to say more, Vivi pulled her sneakers out of her bag and shoved her feet inside. Then she began gathering up the few things of hers scattered around the apartment and tossing them in on top.

"Oh, that's mature," he said, mostly to her back as she stomped around.

She made a rude hand gesture in return.

"And, oh, so ladylike. If people knew the real you they'd think twice before relying so heavily on your opinions and judgments of other people."

She grabbed her coat, shoved her arms inside, and then spun around to level a steely look at him. "At least people *can* rely on me. They can trust me. I'm honest, and I care. That's a lot more than I can say about you." Vivi looked him up and down, then shook her head. "You're a great musician, Connor, but you're a lousy human being."

Hitching her bag over her shoulder, Vivi grabbed her wings and slammed out the door. A moment later he heard the security door at the bottom of the stairs slam shut as well.

Connor couldn't remember a time when he'd been this angry at another person. Oh, he could remember plenty of times being this angry with Vivi, but this level couldn't be reached with anyone else. He splashed another two fingers of Gabe's excellent and expensive Scotch into a glass and tossed it back in one swallow.

So much for that. To think that Vivi could harbor that much distrust and old grudges after everything that had happened recently. And to automatically believe the absolute worst about him. It was insulting. Infuriating.

And it hurt, too.

If anyone had been played for a fool it was him. He'd thought… Well, he'd thought this was more than it had actually turned out to be, and that just rubbed salt in the wound.

He'd brought it on himself, though. He should have known getting involved with Vivi would be a disaster. And, hey, he'd have been right. In less than forty-five minutes they'd gone from lovers to enemies. And now he was beginning to think she'd always been his enemy, and this was just a grand plot on her part to inflict some new misery into his life.

And when she'd stormed out the door…

Damn it, Vivi had just stormed out into the biggest street party in the country in the middle of the night— alone. Between the drunks and the type of people who preyed on the drunks it simply wasn't safe.

He wasn't that big of a jerk.

He stepped out onto the balcony, searching for her in the crowd below, but she was already gone.

Vivi locked the gallery door behind her and reset the alarm. She dropped the stupid wings to the floor in disgust. There was no way on earth she was fighting her way through that mess out there to get home.

Of course she hadn't planned to go home tonight at all. But somehow she'd managed to end up in a shouting match, saying really horrible things, and she had no idea how she'd got there.

The details were a bit fuzzy—the result of letting temper and pride rule the day instead of her brain.

That had been ugly, but those were things that had needed to be said. Connor hadn't changed a bit, and she'd been foolish to pretend otherwise. Angie, whatever her catty reasons for doing so, had been honest with her. Her own willingness to dismiss that information only made the foolishness worse.

There was a bottle of champagne in the fridge in her office, a Christmas gift that she'd never taken home, and that knowledge drew her to her office like a magnet. She didn't feel much like celebrating, but alcohol would dull the current pain. Connor's words had sliced her, but the realization that he just might be right about her deepened the cuts and poured salt in the wound.

She had no one to blame but herself. She'd fallen for Connor's line. The shame came from how easily she'd done it simply because it was so attractive. She'd thought she was breaking new personal ground—

growing as a person, trying new things—but that just seemed like a weak excuse now.

She hated feeling weak. And she hated Connor a little more for being the one to ferret out that weakness and exploit it.

The cork popped out with ease, and Vivi didn't bother looking for a glass. Drinking straight from the bottle—even if it was champagne instead of something harder—seemed to fit her mood. She hugged the bottle to her chest as she curled into the corner of the couch in her office to berate herself and mope. From the depths of her bag she heard her phone chime as a text came in.

Whatever it is, I'm not interested.

Then, with a sigh, she dug the phone out anyway— only to stop short when she saw Connor's name. The message was brief: *At least let me know you made it home.*

What had she expected? An apology? Of course not. And she couldn't—*wouldn't*—read anything into the message. No matter how much she tried to convince him otherwise, he just wouldn't believe she could handle herself on the bad streets of their hometown. Obviously he thought she was weak, too, and it fueled both her anger and her self-flagellation.

Ignore it. She certainly didn't owe Connor anything. Even as she thought it, though, her thumbs were moving over the screen: *I am safely indoors.* There was no need to offer the information that she'd only gone as far as the gallery—just in case Connor decided he wasn't finished with the conversation.

She spent a restless, miserable night on the couch, and when the cathedral bells began to chime for the first Ash Wednesday services she dragged herself home through the nearly empty streets.

Surprisingly, Lorelei was already up. From the pained look and dark bags under her eyes to the aspirin in her hands and the careful, unsteady walk, Lorelei was a living picture of a bad hangover.

"Mercy, Vivi, what happened to you? You look worse than I feel."

Vivi took a deep breath. All the justifications and condemnations she'd arrived at during a mostly sleepless night scrambled to the tip of her tongue, ready to flay Connor.

She burst into tears instead.

TWELVE

—

Good to his word, Connor didn't leave the apartment for several days. He told himself that he needed to work, and he did, getting more accomplished in those days than he had in weeks. Months, probably. It was amazing how productive he could be when he didn't have all kinds of distractions.

His first major accomplishment involved firing Angie shortly after she appeared on Wednesday afternoon. Her somewhat smug acceptance of the condensed and sanitized story of Vivi's departure and her less than enthusiastic response to his decisions about his career clearly showed they'd reached the end of their usefulness to each other.

But throwing himself into his plans only kept the demons at bay for a while, and it didn't taken long for the walls to close in on him. He'd had such a high profile the last few weeks that any absence led to speculation, and his first couple of forays out into the public quickly hit the star-watching blogs—complete with questions about Vivi's sudden absence and what it might mean.

Vivi's words and Vivi's absence haunted him. After a few days he realized she'd been partly right. He'd fired Angie rather than continuing to let her use him as a cash cow, and it had forced him to recognize Vivi's hurt at the possibility he'd used her in a similar fashion. The kernel of truth was there—however small—and had the tables been turned he'd probably feel the same way.

But the fact she'd assumed the worst, rushed to judgment and condemnation... That was just messed up. They might not have the best track record, but that quick jump to believing the worst was uncalled for. *She* was the one who'd made noise about where they were going until he'd started to think that way as well. Now that that had bitten him in the ass, he was discovering he was more than just a little bitter about it.

He was honest enough with himself to realize that the strange hollow feeling in his chest had Vivi's name all over it, and the black irony of the situation didn't escape him. The one woman he'd never thought he'd want to have was the one woman who turned out to be the person who'd made him the happiest. The one woman whose opinion seemed to matter the most didn't like the man he was.

Vivi didn't want him, didn't need him, and didn't trust him. He sat at the piano, his hands wandering aimlessly over the keys, and realized that it mattered a hell of a lot more than it should. Because, if nothing else, the last few weeks had given him a whole new perspective on Vivi—a new appreciation for the woman she was.

And she didn't think he was worth it.

It was a blow to his ego and his pride.

Unable to focus, he took his coffee to the balcony. Two days ago, he'd rearranged the furniture so that all the chairs faced the other way. It gave him a different view, but more important it kept him from staring at the door of Vivi's gallery as if life was a bad, broody music video. He'd seen her a couple of times entering or leaving the gallery, but she never looked up in his direction.

While Vivi hadn't dropped out of the public spotlight, she was definitely keeping a low profile, refusing to comment on Connor's whereabouts or their sudden lack of public togetherness. As far as he could tell Vivi, had simply decided to pretend he didn't exist.

And why did that bother him so much?

He'd made a heap of money singing about this moment, this feeling—even if he'd never truly experienced it before, never wanted to get emotionally involved with anyone before, *ever*. And now he knew why. It sucked. Once he got over it, though, he'd probably make a boatload more money from the songs he would write. He snorted. The whole music industry was predicated on the misery of failed relationships.

Damn it, he didn't *want* to suffer for his art or any of that crap. It was pathetic and ridiculous and shameful, but he wanted Vivi. He wanted that feeling of ease and contentment that came from being with her. He missed her smile and the way she rolled her eyes at him when he said something stupid, and the way she grounded him in reality when he started believing his own press releases.

He wanted Vivi to want him the way he wanted her. He wanted Vivi to love him.

Because he was in love with her.

He sighed and let his head fall back. Great timing figuring that out.

Or maybe it wasn't.

He might have been a little slow getting to this point, but she'd hated him for twenty-something years and managed to come around—*and* she'd come far enough to admit she wanted more. She'd only had a few days to hate him this time, and she didn't know that he was in love with her. He might be able to salvage this.

How was a damn fine question, though.

It wasn't like he could just call her. Even if she deigned to take his call, this was news that needed to be delivered in person. But he had no idea where she was. If he went to the gallery to look for her someone would notice—and the chances of *that* working out well were slim to none.

Which meant his best bet was to call Lorelei.

It took him forever to find her number, and by the time she answered he was feeling more confident about the possibilities.

"It's Connor."

"I know." The clipped words, followed by silence, undermined that confidence a little. She'd always been an ally, but now... Whatever Vivi had told her, it had turned Lorelei against him as well. He'd really screwed this up.

"Do you know where Vivi is?"

"Of course."

Sisterly loyalties were obviously stronger than he'd thought. This was going to be worse than pulling teeth. But this was nothing compared to the reception he expected from Vivi, so it would be good practice.

"Could you tell me where she is?"

"I *could,*" she stressed, "but why on earth would I *want* to?"

"Because it's really, really important that I talk to her."

"Let me save you some time, Connor. She doesn't want to talk to you."

"I just need to tell her something. Please, Lorelei?"

"Why don't you give me the message and I'll pass it along."

He wanted to bang his head against something hard. It would probably be easier in the long run to sit on her front porch until she came home. It would be very public, and possibly very messy, but it might still be preferable to this.

No, if it got ugly, he didn't want it on the blogs. "It's not that kind of message."

"Then, no. I'm not going to let you hurt her more. You've done enough damage."

"And I want to fix it."

"Really?" Lorelei's voice held interest for the first time in this conversation and it buoyed his hopes.

"Yes. That's why I need to find her. To apologize and

tell her that I—" He stopped himself. If he was going to say the words, he should say them to Vivi first. He rubbed his temples, feeling like a complete idiot right now. "There's something she needs to know."

Lorelei thought for a moment, and he hoped that meant he was winning her over. When she spoke, he heaved a sigh of relief. "She's got a ton going on today—"

That figured.

"—but she should be home by five-thirty or six, maybe?"

He didn't want to wait that long. "Where is she now, Lorelei?"

"It's that important, huh? All righty, then." He thought he could hear a smile. "She has meetings this morning—Arts Council, maybe?—then a luncheon of some sort. She'll be at your mom's at three, of course—"

"My mom's?"

"Oh, how quickly we forget. It's the third Thursday of the month. That's the Musical Association meeting."

Of course.

"That'll work. Thanks, Lorelei."

Her voice turned deadly serious. "Don't screw this up. If you hurt her, I will strangle you with Mardi Gras beads and throw your body in the bayou. Understand?"

"Perfectly."

She laughed. "I'm actually looking forward to this meeting now. Good luck."

Lorelei hung up, and Connor felt optimistic for the first time in days. Vivi would be tougher to win over, but Lorelei wouldn't have provided the information if she didn't believe Connor had something to say that Vivi would *want* to hear. That boded well.

He had a couple of hours to figure out what he was going to say and how he was going to do it. He knew the when and the where, but beyond that... His brain went blank.

Lorelei's words came back to him: *Don't screw this up.*

He had to do this right.

For the first time ever, he had a bout of stage fright.

Vivi wanted to care about what Mrs. Gilroy was saying about the annual Musical Association Ball, but honestly she couldn't manage to pay attention—much less dredge up enough of a damn to offer anything to the conversation. From the looks Mrs. Gilroy kept giving her, Vivi had to guess that she was surprised she had so little to say.

But the truth was Vivi didn't care about centerpieces or invitation lists. She didn't care about the budget or potential donors. She didn't even care that Mrs. Mansfield had promised her famous *petit fours* after the business meeting.

She just didn't care. About anything.

She'd tried the time-honored tradition of ice cream and mindless TV, but that had only provided time for self-recrimination and painful moping. Coming face-to-face with the fact she was sanctimonious, supercilious, uptight and everything else Connor had called her was downright depressing. She deserved every bit of the pain she was feeling and had no one to blame but herself that she'd screwed this up so bad.

So she'd gone the opposite route, covering herself in work in the hopes it would keep her busy enough not to think and possibly redeem herself at the same time. Even adding three new committees to her schedule hadn't filled the empty spaces. All it did was occupy her time and exhaust her enough to sleep at night.

But it didn't mean anything or fill her with any satisfaction. She felt like a fraud.

She didn't want to go home, but she certainly didn't want to sit here in Connor's mother's parlor under the gaze of twenty women who all knew she'd been involved with Connor and were dying to ask questions that etiquette mandated were none of their business. Mrs. Mansfield kept giving her long, inscrutable looks from her seat under a picture of Connor at his high school graduation.

I should have just skipped this meeting.

Her mom, showing clairvoyance, patted her knee under the table and gave a small squeeze of support. On her left Lorelei, unbelievably, looked enraptured by the discussion of the possibility of a "Winter Wonderland" theme. Aside from the ridiculous fact the Musical Association Ball would be held in the sweltering heat of August, same as it had been for the last thirty-five years, Lorelei hadn't given the ball a second thought since her presentation seven years ago. She only came to these meetings because Mom expected her to, so this newfound interest in the Association's business was a new development.

Vivi gave herself a strong mental slap and sat up straight in her chair with the intent of listening to Mrs. Gilroy and coming up with something constructive to add. Like it or not, *this* was her life. Connor had been an interlude, a fling, a stray outside of the norm. Like all experiences, it had something to teach her—mainly about the dangers of straying outside the norm.

But the norm was very hard to find now. Not giving a damn about Connor beyond the fact she couldn't stand him *was* the norm, and it was nearly impossible to get back to that state of being. It was the first challenge of her life that didn't hold excitement or appeal. She didn't even want to try.

Her best hope was that time would help. She'd overheard Mrs. Mansfield tell Mrs. Raines that Connor would be going back to L.A. sooner than expected to take care of some business. To Vivi, that had felt like a slap, but she knew that not having Connor around, staying just yards from her gallery's door, would be good for her in the long run.

If that didn't work... Moving to a different city herself was an option under serious consideration as well.

Through the jumble of her thoughts Vivi heard the magic words "meeting adjourned." The ladies of the Musical Association headed for the sideboard *en masse*. Vivi leaned toward her mother. "I'm going to leave now. My allergies are giving me a splitting headache."

Lorelei turned toward her and frowned. "You don't have allergies."

"Well, something is giving me a headache."

Mom stepped in. "Go home and lie down, Vivi. I hope you feel better."

"Good afternoon, ladies. I hear my mom made *petit fours*."

The silence that fell in the wake of Connor's entrance was total as the matriarchs of New Orleans society swiveled their heads to Connor and then to Vivi.

"Connor, sweetheart." Mrs. Mansfield swept forward to give her only son a hug. "This is certainly a surprise."

On cue, everyone started speaking again—slightly louder than necessary in an uncomfortable attempt to seem normal. Her mom's lips pulled into a tight line and she stepped closer to Vivi. Lorelei was grinning like a fool. Everyone else was ignoring her—except Connor, who seemed to be trying to stare her into the floor even as he greeted the women who pressed forward to see him. The ice that had formed around her feet at the sound of Connor's voice felt impossible to break, and Vivi's pulse jumped as adrenaline surged through her veins.

Connor's voice sounded unnaturally loud. "I remember when Mom used to make me come and play for Association meetings. I thought it might be fun to do it without being forced."

"For once." Mrs. Mansfield smiled with pride. "That would be wonderful."

Connor moved to the piano, and the women seemed to be back in their seats instantly. Only Vivi remained standing. Leaving now would only call attention to herself and embarrass her. She gave the universe the chance to grant her wish and let the floor swallow her, but when that didn't happen, she sank carefully into her chair with what she hoped looked like poise.

The need to strangle Connor felt comfortably familiar, and actually helped tame her racing heart. She felt her mother's hand slide under hers in support, and then, unbelievably, Lorelei did the same from the other side.

Connor played a quick progression of notes. "Trust my mom to keep it in perfect tune."

Mrs. Mansfield looked ready to burst with pride and pleasure.

"This is the Musical Association, so I should probably play some Chopin or Liszt. If I remember correctly, Mrs. Gilroy loves Rachmaninoff." He played a few bars.

Now Mrs. Gilroy had the same expression as Mrs. Mansfield. Vivi focused her eyes on an oil painting above the piano and took slow breaths.

"But I'm a bit out of practice on the classics, ladies—sorry. I'm actually here to get your collective and esteemed opinion on a new piece I've been working on."

Vivi could feel the pleasure of the members. *Spare me.* Connor had these women eating out of the palms of his very talented hands. She knew the feeling.

"It's actually a song inspired by our own Vivienne LaBlanc."

A gasp fluttered though the crowd.

"We've spent quite a lot of time together the last few weeks, as you know."

I hate him. Did he have to have the last word, humiliating her in front of people she'd known her entire life? *If I ever get out of here, I'm moving to a cabin in Wisconsin.*

"It's funny how coming home can bring you full circle. One of the first songs I ever wrote was for Vivi. We were in junior high and, while the rest of the class enjoyed it, it didn't go over very well with Vivi herself."

No, I'll kill him first, and then move to Wisconsin.

"I hope she likes this one a bit better."

Vivi was so focused on not looking at him, not completely losing it in front of all these people, that the music didn't register at first. Then shock moved through her. Sixteen notes that she knew by heart. The sixteen notes that he'd taught her that first night they were together.

She remembered sitting inside the circle of his arms while he helped her find the keys, and then the way he'd made the music around her. The memory brought a physical sensation that bordered on pain. Her eyes began to burn, and she quickly swallowed the lump forming in her throat.

Look at me, what do you see?
A man, longing to be free.

Connor's voice rolled over the room like a rich blanket, and pain streaked through her soul.

Free to be, true to you,
To the end.

Vivi could feel twenty pairs of eyes on her, but she refused to take *her* eyes off the painting above the piano.

I'll listen close and understand.
To the end.

The music grew louder and Connor's voice grew stronger.
I dare you to hold me.
One touch and you'll never know lonely again.

Although she didn't want to, Vivi couldn't stop herself from risking a peek at Connor. His eyes bored straight into hers.

Again and again, we'll just be—
To the end.

Vivi's feet finally unfroze, and she moved quickly to the door. She was nearly blinded by the tears in her eyes, but she made it down the porch stairs without falling and headed for the gate.

Connor caught her before she had it open.

"Vivi, where are you going?"

"Anywhere but here. I can't believe you just did that."

Connor's eyes went wide. "That? *That* was my attempt at an apology."

Vivi had been hit with too many things in the last few minutes. She said the first thing that came to mind. "You had to do it in front of the Musical Association?"

There was an awkward pause. "Well, you don't have a piano at your house." He half smiled at her. "And I didn't think I could get you to come to Gabe's. This was the only place."

His earlier words finally filtered through. "Wait. That was an apology? To me?"

"Yeah. It's still a little rough in places, but I generally do better with words set to music."

"An apology?" She couldn't quite wrap her head around it.

"For being a jerk. For not being honest with you— not at the beginning, and not the other night."

She couldn't quite keep up. "About what the other night?"

"If I'd been honest, I'd have told you that I love you."

The world swam for a moment. When it righted, Vivi couldn't believe she'd heard him correctly. "That doesn't make sense."

He nodded. "You're right. And yet the weird thing is that it still manages to be true. I don't know why I didn't figure that out years ago." Shrugging that off, he reached for her hands. "Of course, you've never accused me of being particularly intelligent."

"But…"

"I don't understand it either, Vivi. All I know is that you are the strongest woman I've ever met. You're smart and beautiful and you don't let anyone—including me—stand in your way. You care and you have a good heart. You make me want to be the kind of man who deserves that kind of woman."

Her breath caught in her chest and her lungs squeezed her heart in a vise. His words made her actions the other night all the more inexcusable. "I'm the one who owes *you* an apology. I was way out of line and I overreacted."

"All things considered, though…it's understandable."

"I'm still really sorry."

"Me, too. Old habits die hard."

"Yeah." Then she looked up at him. "But is it weird to say that I'm happy anyway?"

"Not at all." He rubbed his hands over her arms. "You know what would make *me* happy, though?"

"What?"

He cleared his throat. "I said something kind of big and important a second ago, and you haven't said it back. The suspense is bordering on painful."

Her heart gave another small squeeze. "For someone who's made a lot of money—and made a lot of women swoon—with love songs, you're a little unknowledgeable of the particulars. If I didn't love you—hadn't loved you—I wouldn't have cared what you said or did."

"Really?" Connor looked quite pleased.

She returned the smile. "Really."

"Good, because I'm realizing I'm a bit of a sore loser, too. At least when it comes to losing you."

Connor's mouth found hers, and Vivi felt whole for the first time. It didn't make sense, but that didn't make it any less right.

The sound of applause brought her back to reality. Heat rising in her cheeks, she peeked over Connor's shoulder to see the entire Musical Association membership crowded on the Mansfields' front porch.

"Do you always draw an audience?" she asked.

"It happens." Connor laced his fingers through hers and squeezed her hand. "You know, there's a whole other verse to that song. Want to hear it?"

"Maybe later. If you hadn't noticed, I was on my way out when you stopped me."

Connor's smile dimmed slightly. "Oh? Where are you going?"

"Wherever you're willing to take me."

That brought back Connor's smile, and it carried a promise that sent shivers down to the soles of her feet. Opening the gate, he pulled her through without so much as a farewell glance at the ladies on the porch.

His car was parked at the curb, and the lights blinked as they approached. Opening the door, Connor gave her a quick kiss and a wink. "Then you better hold on to your halo, Saint Vivi."

"Saints and Sinners is over," she told him. "You even got the trophy."

"Forget the trophy. I got the girl. And that's far better."

Her heart turned gooey and melty at his words. Connor helped her into the front seat and then got in the other side. As the engine roared to life he reached out to take her hand. He was right: it might be crazy, but it still made perfect sense.

"I was right. There were no losers in this competition."

"I wholeheartedly agree."

A thought flashed across her brain and it must have shown on her face, because Connor looked at her funny. "What's wrong, Vivi?"

I can't. I shouldn't. But he was the one who'd brought it up.

"If we're both winners, and you only wanted the girl anyway...?"

"Yes...?" he prompted.

"Can *I* have the trophy?"

Connor was laughing as he kissed her.

* * * * *

REQUEST YOUR FREE BOOKS!
2 FREE NOVELS PLUS 2 FREE GIFTS!

❧ HARLEQUIN®

Romance

From the Heart, For the Heart

YES! Please send me 2 FREE Harlequin® Romance novels and my 2 FREE gifts (gifts are worth about $10). After receiving them, if I don't wish to receive any more books, I can return the shipping statement marked "cancel." If I don't cancel, I will receive 6 brand-new novels every month and be billed just $4.09 per book in the U.S. or $4.49 per book in Canada. That's a savings of at least 14% off the cover price! It's quite a bargain! Shipping and handling is just 50¢ per book in the U.S. and 75¢ per book in Canada.* I understand that accepting the 2 free books and gifts places me under no obligation to buy anything. I can always return a shipment and cancel at any time. Even if I never buy another book, the two free books and gifts are mine to keep forever.

114/314 HDN FVR7

Name	(PLEASE PRINT)	
Address		Apt. #
City	State/Prov.	Zip/Postal Code

Signature (if under 18, a parent or guardian must sign)

Mail to the **Harlequin**® Reader Service:
IN U.S.A.: P.O. Box 1867, Buffalo, NY 14240-1867
IN CANADA: P.O. Box 609, Fort Erie, Ontario L2A 5X3

**Are you a subscriber to Harlequin Romance books
and want to receive the larger-print edition?
Call 1-800-873-8635 or visit www.ReaderService.com.**

* Terms and prices subject to change without notice. Prices do not include applicable taxes. Sales tax applicable in N.Y. Canadian residents will be charged applicable taxes. Offer not valid in Quebec. This offer is limited to one order per household. Not valid for current subscribers to Harlequin Romance books. All orders subject to credit approval. Credit or debit balances in a customer's account(s) may be offset by any other outstanding balance owed by or to the customer. Please allow 4 to 6 weeks for delivery. Offer available while quantities last.

Your Privacy—The Harlequin® Reader Service is committed to protecting your privacy. Our Privacy Policy is available online at www.ReaderService.com or upon request from the Harlequin Reader Service.

We make a portion of our mailing list available to reputable third parties that offer products we believe may interest you. If you prefer that we not exchange your name with third parties, or if you wish to clarify or modify your communication preferences, please visit us at www.ReaderService.com/consumerschoice or write to us at Harlequin Reader Service Preference Service, P.O. Box 9062, Buffalo, NY 14269. Include your complete name and address.

FIRST TIME FOR EVERYTHING

by Aimee Carson

Her leg stilled, and she adopted a wide-eyed, innocent air. "I still haven't addressed the age-old question—boxers or briefs?"

"I wouldn't classify that as an age-old question," he said, and the corner of his eyes crinkled as he smiled.

Blinking hard, Jax stared at him. She'd thought it had been a fluke, but her first impression had been spot-on. He was extra hot when humored.

Fascinated, she continued. "Sure it is. Ranks right up there with the argument over which is more influential, nature or nurture."

Intense interest flared in his face. "I wasn't aware men's underwear were as hotly contested as genes versus environment in forming personality."

"In certain circles it is," she said.

A droll skepticism crossed his face. "None that I frequent."

"That's not saying much. And as far as DNA and environment are concerned...I've always believed we're a unique combination of the two."

Pursing his lips, his voice turned thoughtful. "I've always hoped we could overcome them both."

Intriguing response. Very intriguing.

Troubled by the notion, she studied his scar, wondering about its origin. "Is that why you wear a suit? To overcome your DNA?"

The twinkle in his eyes grew brighter. "A better question would be, is psychoanalysis via underwear a required course as a music therapist?"

Amused, Jax swept a stray hair from her cheek. "No. But every choice you make reveals a little of your character. You're definitely a briefs man. You like everything neatly—" she lifted her gaze to his for effect *"—contained."*

A quick flash of a devilish grin morphed outrageously handsome to downright devastating, and the euphoric high it produced only made her miss the smile more when it was gone. Disturbed by the thought, she sent him a pointed look, and her voice lost the teasing tone. "Including your emotions."

His scar shifted in surprise at her blunt statement, and she was almost ashamed she felt so smug about bringing the man down a notch.

Apparently, he didn't agree.

"I think I'll let the insinuation my emotions are contained in my underwear pass without comment," he finally said. His faint smile was concerning. "Especially since my deal with my sister includes further contact with you."

Confused, and more than a little alarmed, Jax frowned.

"Yes, in exchange for me helping you, she promised me she'd finally let me hire someone to move in with us and help her with her daily activities until she's out of her cast."

"And how does that affect *me?*"

He settled back and shot her a Master Of All He Surveyed smile. "Because the live-in caretaker is going to be you."

Look out for FIRST TIME FOR EVERYTHING by Aimee Carson. Available February 19 2013, wherever Harlequin books are sold.

HARLEQUIN®

KISS™

Use this coupon to
SAVE $1.00
on the purchase of
ANY 2
Harlequin KISS books.

Available wherever books are sold, including most
bookstores, supermarkets, drugstores and discount stores.

---✂-----

SAVE $1.00 ON THE PURCHASE OF **ANY TWO** HARLEQUIN KISS BOOKS.

Coupon expires July 31, 2013. Redeemable at participating retail outlets
in the U.S. and Canada only. Limit one coupon per customer.

Return to New Orleans with the LaBlanc Sisters

AVAILABLE FEB 19!

THE TAMING OF A WILD CHILD

by *USA Today* Bestselling author Kimberly Lang

Waking up in a stranger's bed is not how socialite Lorelei LaBlanc planned on spending the morning after the night before. From now on, she's determined to have no more secret hookups with Donovan St. James—he's a journalist and she's perfect tabloid material....

www.Harlequin.com